Jack looked at the three sooty faces: Bál nodding, resolute; Ruth shaking her head, terrified; Sardâr grimacing, pained. He looked through the second-story window at the pavement below.

They jumped.

Perhaps naturally for someone who'd grown up on a steady diet of James Bond and *Die Hard*, Jack still retained some faith that leaping several meters down onto stone would be fine and would not hurt. It wasn't, and it did.

He hit the ground on his side and heard a couple of snaps, nuclear agony exploding across his upper body. He had spent three weeks in combat training, been hit by Dark alchemical lightning, and journeyed in and out of a volcano, and this still factored high on the pain scale. He tried to pull himself to his feet but was unable. He couldn't move his left arm at all, and even lifting his neck shot arrows across his nerves.

All he could see were the boots of those navy-coated men marching towards them. Ruth and Bál's explanations turned to cries of protest as they were hauled to the wagon. The dwarf's struggle was proving too much for the captor, but Bál was soon restrained by several more whilst one beat him to his knees with a truncheon.

Jack recognized his own voice shouting just as he felt a force on his shoulders. He was being dragged across the road towards the same wagon, his wounded arm scraping the street.

Contents

james bartholomeusz

the black rose

The Seven Stars Trilogy

MEDALLION

P R E S S

Medallion Press, Inc.
Printed in USA

For Grandma Marina

Published 2012 by Medallion Press, Inc.
The MEDALLION PRESS LOGO
is a registered trademark of Medallion Press, Inc.

Typeset in Gentium
Printed in the United States of America

ISBN 9781605425375
10 9 8 7 6 5 4 3 2 1

First Edition

Part III

"Surely some revelation is at hand;
Surely the Second Coming is at hand"

"The Second Coming"
W. B. Yeats

Chapter I
a tale of two cities

There came a knock at the door. The woman took a last look out of the window at the street below and, in the most refined way, seated herself on the high sofa. Beside her, a girl sat fluttering a willow-patterned fan. She was slight with Middle Eastern features, and though her face was encased in many layers of makeup, she appeared underfed and ill. Like a fragile porcelain doll, she wore an absurdly curved corset of ivory and teal and similar dainty gloves. Her eyes, unfocused, stared into the middle distance, seemingly unaware of anything around her.

"Enter," the woman called.

The double doors opposite the sofa swung open.

A butler, clothed from head to foot in an ornate tailcoat, waistcoat, trousers, shirt, and cravat, cleared his throat. "A Mister Frederick Goodwin, of Goodwin

Construction Limited, madame."

"Bring him in."

The butler bowed and backed out.

The woman took a moment to ensure everything was in order. The floral wallpaper clashed horribly with the decorated drapes. The carpet, so detailed with diamonds and leaves, offended any possible sense of aesthetics. Behind her hung a dull portrait of an austere old man, barely discernible against a muddy backdrop. A glass of water, three-quarters full as if the occupant had actually been drinking, occupied a small wooden table to the porcelain girl's left. Yes, everything was in order.

The doors opened a second time, now to reveal an enormous middle-aged man. The butler held out his hands and received a face full of hat and traveling cloak as the guest strode in. His cane, alabaster white, clipped the carpet with every step he took towards the armchair. Receiving a nod of invitation from the woman, he seated his vastness upon the overstuffed cushions and laid his cane on the table next to him.

"Lady Osborne, so glad that we could finally meet face-to-face." By the manner in which he leaned forward, he evidently expected her to offer her hand. When she did not move, he reached into one of his pockets and produced a pack of papers. From another pocket he drew a monocle, which he affixed to one eye. He leafed through the documents. "I must confess, Your Ladyship, I was surprised at your letter. The components you have requested are, *ahem*, quite unusual."

"As I explained in my letter, Mister Goodwin, His

Lordship was explicit in his instructions."

"Yes . . . have you any idea when Lord Osborne is due to return?"

The woman pursed her lips. "No, I am afraid not, Mister Goodwin. He may be indisposed for quite some time."

Mister Goodwin found the correct document and pulled it out of the stack, placing it on the low coffee table. He set a fountain pen next to it, indicating the space she was meant to sign. "I must ask *again*, Your Ladyship, if it is not too much of an impertinence, whether you require *these very specific* components . . ."

"Yes, Mister Goodwin," the woman replied coldly, scribbling her signature on the line.

He took back the sheet, giving her a long, appraising look. "Very well," he said finally, tucking the sheet and pen into the pack and replacing them in his pocket. He popped his monocle out, slipped it into his waistcoat, and cleared his throat fussily. "Again, if it is not too much of an impertinence, I must ask if you intend to extend your visit here—"

"It *is* too much of an impertinence, Mister Goodwin." The woman rose. "And besides, my daughter and I are late for an important engagement. Nicolas"—the butler reappeared at the door—"please show our guest out."

Mister Goodwin stood as well. He did not attempt to kiss his hostess's hand this time but nodded at her coolly. "We shall contact you once the bank has accepted the payment, and we then may proceed."

She returned his nod.

He glanced at the girl. She had heeded neither his

arrival nor his presence during the entire visit, her gaze fixed firmly in the middle distance. Mister Goodwin did not quite know what to make of this engagement. In his professional experience, Lord Osborne was not the kind of man to take on an immigrant ward. Mister Goodwin had not even known His Lordship was *married*.

Clearing his throat yet again, he retrieved his alabaster cane from the table and marched out. The door swung shut behind him.

The woman waited for the footsteps to recede down the hallway, then sagged into her seat. Her concentration ebbed, and she let out a sigh that misted as it entered the air.

The temperature of the room was dropping rapidly. Claws of frost grasped at the wallpaper, the sofas, and the tables—every particle of moisture solidified. The contents of the glass froze within seconds. A moment later the glass itself had cracked. The slab of ice shattered on the tabletop.

The signee had also changed. Gone were the ridiculous frills and neurotically patterned flowers. She now wore a black cloak curved to fit her body. Her hair, freed from that ridiculous bun, now hung freely, slanted over one eye. Gone too was the stuffed sofa; she now reclined on a throne of carved ice. Released from the sensory illusion, various arcane devices were now positioned in symmetry around the room, all humming dimly with Dark energy.

She glanced over her shoulder. The painting had vanished, and in its place stood a tall, thin mirror in a gothic arch. The glass was frosted, distorting the reflection of the room and the woman. Only one thing was completely visible. Ghostlike on the other side of the glass, the dark-skinned porcelain girl stared into the middle distance.

The Emperor decided that he was to lead the midnight prayers himself that night, a rarity in itself. As sunlight no longer visited Nexus, the concept of midnight was somewhat defunct, but the times of day were observed nonetheless.

Having blessed the congregation, he left the nave via the screen and proceeded to the crossing. He moved between the pews, gazing upwards at the dark stone archways of the vaulted ceiling. The stained glass windows set high into the walls each depicted a religious scene in candle-reflecting crimson. His boots clicked on the marble floor, the massive rose pattern at the center scattering ornamental thorns into every corner of the room. Incense wavered on the breeze, and the austere notes of the organ resounded behind him like a funeral march.

The imperial throne was mounted on a pedestal behind the altar, flanked by ranks of flickering candles. It was here that the boy had been commanded to wait and, to the Emperor's amusement, he had done exactly this.

The leader of the Cult of Dionysus settled upon the throne and, placing his ceremonially robed arms upon the wings, regarded the figure before him. Even after

5

cleanup the boy looked dishevelled: unruly dark hair spread over his scalp, and red welts marked his limbs and neck from where he had been chained. Nevertheless, he had been given an acolyte's tunic to wear, and those emerald eyes were alive and fierce with resistance.

"Would you consider yourself a religious man, Mister Steele?"

Alex narrowed his gaze but said nothing.

"I take it, then, that you do not."

The boy swallowed and leaned back on the altar. His feet ached from standing up for so long. "I've seen alchemy work. I've seen Light and Darkness battle each other across the universe. I've even seen *into* the Darkness. But no, I haven't seen anything to suggest a god at work."

The Emperor smirked, and Alex thought he saw grey smoke wisp across those yellowed teeth.

"But you lot worship a dragon, don't you?"

The Emperor followed Alex's gaze. The wall against which his throne was mounted was indeed a stone carving of a titanic black dragon, colossal wings spread symmetrically, flames pluming from its mouth, clawed feet planted either side of the seat.

"The Dragon is the essential representation of Darkness: amongst the fluid collective, a single anchor point. Despite our pretensions, this world is still part of the Light—scarcely. Worshippers need a tangible individual icon to focus on." The Emperor grinned. "And incidentally, you have seen *nothing* of the Darkness. Yet."

Alex exhaled, dragging his gaze from the stone dragon's face to the malevolent humanoid one upon the

A Tale of Two Cities

throne. "So why am I here? What's this 'offer'?"

"I am not going to conceal my aims for you, Mister Steele. By the time we are done, you will have changed sides in this war."

"What?" Alex scoffed, equally amazed and amused. "You think you can make me abandon the Apollonians and join the Cult?" At this point, he actually laughed, for the first time since he'd arrived on this planet.

"What makes you think there are only two sides?"

Again Alex thought he saw grey smoke trace about the Emperor.

"I'm a prisoner of war. You're the one keeping me here. Why should I help you?"

The Emperor raised himself from the chair and turned to ponder the candles. "Because I know you better than you do. You are in denial about your past. You've convinced yourself that you belong as a minor agent for a group of vigilantes. I can show you your true potential."

Alex leaned back farther, skeptical. He wasn't about to trust this creature, the leader of the organization he'd spent over a year fighting, and he certainly wasn't taken in by the talk about destiny. But back in the cell, the Emperor *had* known something he'd never disclosed to anyone still living. If nothing else, he needed to discover how the Emperor knew so much. And he might come across information important to the Apollonians in the process. He *would* be a double agent, just not the sort the Emperor had in mind. "Okay, I'll humor you. What were you thinking?"

The Emperor smirked and took Alex by the shoulder, steering him around the altar and onto the main flooring of the crossing. They passed under the vaulted arches and over the black rose, the organ music echoing high above.

Chapter II
reflections and nightmares

Jack awoke with a start. He was, as he now knew he had been all through the nightmare, in his claustrophobic cabin aboard *The Golden Turtle*. His bunk took up an entire wall, raised to accommodate shelves and drawers underneath. An empty square table occupied a corner, and the only other fitting in the room was a tall wardrobe on the opposite wall. A small porthole near his head showcased only the deep gloom of the underwater world they traversed.

He clambered off his bed, his arms easily reaching the ceiling of the cabin. He sagged onto the carpeted floor, stretching out his neck.

Had he not been here, but perhaps back on Earth, he may well have dismissed the last month as some kind of mental breakdown. As it was, traveling in the company of two people who were, unequivocally, an elf and a dwarf made this considerably harder. In these last six weeks, he had been caught up in a sorcerer's attack on his hometown of Birchford, had been transported to another world, had come into contact with races of beings he'd thought existed only in myths and fairy tales, and had twice fought and defeated a giant demon lobster. And his newfound abilities to, amongst others, set things on fire, levitate objects, and generate light from nowhere ended any attempt to explain away his current predicament. He still couldn't quite understand how or why he, a fairly ordinary British teenager, had got into this situation.

When he'd finally been given an explanation for all this madness, it hadn't been disappointing in its magnitude. As far as he could tell, a war was currently being fought between the Apollonians, defenders of the Light, and the Cult of Dionysus, who were in the process of constructing a Dark alchemical superweapon called the Aterosa. Both sides were racing to discover the whereabouts of the Shards of the Risa Star, an extremely powerful object which, if reunited, seemed capable of shaping the outcome of this conflict.

In the times when he hadn't been working around the vessel or in conversation with Bál the dwarf and Sardâr the elf about the Apollonians' plans, four people had chiefly occupied Jack's thoughts. The first, of course, was his closest friend, Lucy. She, out of all who'd become caught up in this war, had been the most constant in her support of him. Their last parting had been heartfelt, and, ever since, he had been staving off the feeling that they should have stayed together. She was now on a parallel but separate journey, in search of a Shard of the Risa Star, alongside two other Apollonians, Hakim and Adâ, both elves, though how near or far away they had gone he did not know. He thought of her mostly because the two of them, if no one else, shared this situation: they had been brought from Earth against their will, had been flung into a world they didn't understand, and both faced the horrors of the Cult. And they had survived, which was no mean feat. There was also the fact that the two hadn't spent over a week apart in the last year. He missed her most of all and could be fairly certain she felt the same way.

Second was, until a few weeks ago, his only other friend, Alex. He had known Alex since his arrival at the orphanage when Jack was seven and he was ten, and the two had remained firm friends ever since. Alex had reappeared the night of the Cult's attack, having been absent from Birchford without explanation for eighteen months. As Jack and Lucy had later discovered, he had been gone not only from their town but from their *planet*, working with the Apollonians in their battle against the Cult. Barely hours back on Earth, Alex had been stabbed and kidnapped by the Cult and was now presumably held captive on the organization's elusive base world of Nexus.

In a solid third place was the captain of *The Golden Turtle*, Ruth Sparrow. Jack had met Ruth minutes after he had left Earth; it was she who had carried him and

Lucy as passengers on her ship to an Apollonian base. That voyage had lasted only three days, and yet they had connected immediately. They were both orphans as far as they knew: he due to his mother's abandonment, she due to amnesia and imprisonment. Ruth was, right now, somewhere else on this world-traversing submarine, probably sleeping. That thought gave him an unusual amount of comfort.

Finally, with these three as miniature suns lighting the inside of his head, the fourth lurked in the shadows behind. Jack had so far met two priests of the Council of Thirteen, which governed the Cult of Nexus: Iago, an old enemy of Sardâr's who had joined the Cult to secure domination of their mutual home world of Tâbesh; and Icarus, about whom Jack now realized he knew next to nothing. It had been Icarus who had led the attack on Birchford, attempted to sacrifice Lucy to release a powerful demon, *and* kidnapped Alex. He had seemed to recognize Jack, and Jack remembered a feeling of déjà-vu when seeing him, as if of someone he had met but never really got to know. And after a brief glimpse into the Cult's plans, he knew the Emperor had assigned Icarus to find another Shard. This couldn't bode well for the Apollonians.

Jack rubbed his eyes. They were beginning to close again. The sweat had faded, and now he was getting cold. He clambered into his bunk. The conditions at his orphanage hadn't been great, considering the sparse funding, but they were considerably better than this.

He lay down and closed his eyes.

Reflections and Nightmares

Ruth was falling into Darkness, suffocating. She twisted around. Behind her, she glimpsed where she had come from, a back alley constructed entirely from alchemical piping and stone slabs. Several windows high above glimmered with artificial light. The sky was wrought with the perpetual storm of this place, lightning splintering the billowing clouds. A portal of dark energy enwrapped her, some invisible force pulling her backwards through it. The image of the alleyway was disappearing, becoming smaller and smaller as if at the end of a telescope. Her senses were gradually shutting down: she could see nothing, barely breathe, hear only the stifling silence of the Darkness . . .

Ruth gasped and sat up in bed, drenched in sweat. She, too, was in a cabin of *The Golden Turtle*, though as captain she had considerably bigger quarters than Jack's. She swung her legs over the bed and dropped down, seating herself at the table bolted to the floor in the center of the room. She pressed a key on the table leg, and an overhead lamp cast an orange hue across the room.

She lay her forearm on the table, palm upwards. A tattoo, a stylized lion in black ink, was woven into her skin just below the elbow. This and the nightmare were the only remnants from her life before *The Golden Turtle*.

Five years previously, she had awoken aboard the ship with no memory of her former life or how she had arrived there. The captain, Ishmael, had told her she'd

the black rose

been hauled out of the sea, unconscious, close to drowning. With nowhere to return to, she had been enlisted in the ship's crew and eventually adopted by Ishmael. It was only later, when she had come into contact with the Cult of Dionysus, that her recurring nightmare began to make sense. She had been imprisoned on Nexus but had somehow fallen or escaped into the Darkness and ended up in another world.

Ruth sat back and gazed up at the lantern's fiery pattern crisscrossing the metal ceiling. Jack, she knew, had had a similar family experience but without a parental figure like Ishmael as a guiding beacon at the end of it. She presumed Jack wanted to return to his home world, but she was secretly glad he was unable to for the time being. Her first proper talk with him, the night he had arrived on *The Golden Turtle*, had been the only time she had opened up to anyone but Ishmael. She considered seeing if he was awake now but dismissed the idea immediately. He wouldn't want to be disturbed at this time.

She stood, turned off the light, and went back to bed.

Jack awoke properly to a knock on the door a few hours later. It was Aonair, a crew member he vaguely knew.

"Sardâr wants you to get to the command deck. We're nearing our destination."

Jack washed quickly, changed into new clothes, and made his way across the ship to the command deck. There was obviously no natural lighting here, as they were underwater, but soft lamps lining the wood-panelled corridors mimicked the cycle of day and night. He passed various crew members and eventually came to the double doors emblazoned with a golden turtle symbol.

This room was a large glassy dome, the head of the turtle, against which the dank water of their current passage pressed on all sides. Futuristic navigational machines lined the walls, operators sitting before the humming screens. In the center, on a lower level, a large oak table was bolted down, with a plethora of maps pinned to it. Three people stood around it. Ruth, adorned with her signature bandana, was directly opposite him; the elf Sardâr, Middle Eastern in complexion and wearing a tunic, studying one of the maps; and Bál the dwarf stood a little back from the others, distinctly out of place in his traveling gear.

Bál's first reaction to *The Golden Turtle* had been a mixture of wonder and gruffness. He came from a world, Thorin Salr, which roughly resembled Earth's Dark Ages. This ultrasophisticated technology had baffled Jack, so he could only imagine how Bál felt.

"Jack." Sardâr gestured for him to join them at the table. "We're due to arrive at Albion tomorrow."

Jack dropped to the level of the table, smiled at Ruth, and got a look at the maps. The one on top, which Sardâr had been examining, showed a city with a river weaving through its center.

"So where is this place?" Bál asked, leaning closer. "What *is* Albion?"

"It seems to be a city-state, which governs the

surrounding lands," Sardâr said. "It is in a stage of rapid development—Jack, roughly in line with your nine-teenth-century Europe—so there's an increasing urban population."

"Do we have any idea where the Shard is?" Ruth asked.

"Not at the moment. We don't know if it's even in the city, though that would seem the most likely place. We'll need to get there and make some inquiries to find out."

"And the Cult?"

"They will be on the same trail. We've got to keep on our guard. As we saw through the black mirror, the Emperor has dispatched Archbishop Nimue to discover the Shard, and she is probably significantly closer than we are."

"So what do we need in the way of disguises? And weapons? And alchemy?" Jack looked around. The only world other than Earth he had visited had been Thorin Salr. As the local population of dwarves had seen only elves and goblins, he and Ruth had been disguised as elves with *The Golden Turtle*'s technology. Those disguises had been reverted as soon as they'd returned to the ship, and he was still getting used to his human body. He wasn't too keen on transforming again anytime soon. "How are we going to stop drawing attention to ourselves?"

"From what we know, the local population is human—so, Jack, you're fine."

Jack breathed an inaudible sigh of relief.

"Bál, you and I are going to need some alchemical disguising."

The dwarf grimaced. Not alone amongst his fellows, he had reacted with a strong distaste to alchemy when the Apollonians and then the Cult had brought it to his home world. Though his experience with the First Shard had changed that somewhat, he was still none too keen on the idea.

"What about me?" Ruth put in. "I mean, I look human, but from what I know about the history of Jack's world, I'm not going to fit in very well with this skin color."

"We'll sort something out," Sardâr replied. "You may be surprised at the tolerance." The elf stood and went over to inquire with one of the operators about the journey.

"So you're coming with us, then?" Jack addressed Ruth.

"That's the plan. The ship will keep a low profile under the river whilst we search. We might need to get out quickly at any time."

Sardâr returned to them. "Alchemy, in Albion, is rare, possibly unknown. But if we don't want to draw the attention of the authorities, then we'll need it: we won't be carrying weapons."

"No weapons!" Bál looked outraged. His axe, his companion throughout the siege on his home world, had barely left his side on the journey.

"None. We may pick some up whilst we're there, but in any case, you've got the First Shard to learn how to use now." Sardâr raised his eyebrows, looking at the chain around Bál's neck on which a Shard of the Risa Star hung. Jack instinctively reached around his own neck for the familiar thread on which another Shard, the Seventh, was looped.

The dwarf managed to grumble himself into silence.

"If that's all," Sardâr concluded, "then I think we should get back to work. I'm sure Quentin has some duties for us all to perform."

Ruth's quivering first mate stood at the command deck door, evidently looking for some potential recruits for a job.

Being royalty on his home world, Bál hadn't been impressed with having to pitch in with menial work like everyone else. He rolled his eyes and followed Jack to the door.

Reflections and Nightmares

Chapter III
snow and water

Lucy had never been so cold. She was trudging across a ridge, knee-deep in settled snow. To her left, an imposing cliff rose, slate grey but with ice clinging in stalactites to the nooks and crevasses. To her right, the ground fell away in a steep slope to a frozen river that reflected the pale sunlight and a sparkling white plain that might once have been agricultural lands. Beyond that, mountains rose from the frosted fog: bleak, pale regents marking the horizon. It was from those regents that the wind sliced, surging like a wave of invisible arrows across the plains towards them.

They had been here for less than a day, but already she'd had enough. She had changed for the better over the last month—she accepted that—but her body still had its limits. Recovering a childhood knowledge of martial arts to defend a fortress against demons was one thing; hiking through a mountain range with no end in sight was entirely another. One of the first Apollonians she had met, Vince, had arrived from Earth in his dimension ship the day after she had watched Jack depart on *The Golden Turtle*. The journey from Thorin Salr to here—this wasteland was called the Sveta Mountains, according to the others—had, like her first journey from Earth, induced extreme nausea. Now it was the cold, fatigue, and hunger which were taking their toll.

Vince was in front of her, plowing through so that she could follow in his footsteps. In an arctic jacket, thick boots, and trapper hat, he was far better equipped for the weather than the rest were. She, Adâ, and Hakim had left Thorin Salr with the best attire that could be provided, though it was hardly suitable for this climate. She was mostly wrapped in assorted furs and thick hides, though the wind and damp snow seemed to have found the gaps and slid in to nestle. The two elves were behind her, Hakim's wooden staff leaving an additional print in the snow every few feet.

Ahead, the ridge narrowed, and their path took them between two high rocks. Vince clambered up first and disappeared over the top. Lucy followed but slipped down the bank on the other side. Picking herself up and shaking the residual snow off her clothes, she followed Vince's gaze. The land dropped steadily before them, plateauing into an ivory plain. The river wove like a shimmering ribbon draped across a white sheet. Beyond it, she could make out a cluster of dark shapes, apparently alone in the wilderness.

Snow and Water

"Are those . . . houses?" She gasped, her breath clouding.

"Yep," Vince replied, his eyes still fixed on them. "Well, huts. A settlement, anyway."

"Who would live *here*?"

"Goblins, I believe," Hakim responded, joining them. "Similar to the ones who live around Thorin Salr, though I'd wager not exactly the same. Life never evolves exactly the same on different worlds."

"It's probably a good thing we don't have any dwarves here then," Lucy replied.

Adâ smirked.

One of the more surprising developments in the last week had been the uncomfortable peace agreed between the previously opposed dwarf and goblin populations of Thorin Salr. The two had united to fight off the Cult, but that didn't mean things were neatly parcelled up. Even though Bál, one of the most vocally xenophobic dwarves, had voiced his support for the peace agreement, no one was naïve enough to think all on both sides felt the same way.

"So is that where we're going?" Lucy asked.

"It certainly looks like it," Hakim replied. "With this few people living here, there's a good chance those goblins can at least point us towards the Fifth Shard. And, for that matter, the Cult."

Vince began down the slope, tilted sideways to avoid falling.

Pulling her furs tighter to resist the slicing wind, Lucy followed.

the black rose

True to Sardâr's prediction, *The Golden Turtle* arrived at Albion the following night. Jack had no indication of them drawing near, as they kept underwater all the way, but he heeded the elf's call to disembark when it finally came.

He returned to his room and repacked his few possessions in the sack he had taken from Thorin Salr, laying out the three remaining items on the table. The first was a gauntlet, a gift from the goblin Vodnik for Jack's part in saving him and his comrades during the battle. The second was the language ring, another alchemical contraption originating from *The Golden Turtle*, which translated other languages to him as if they were actually being spoken in English. The third, and most important, was the Seventh Shard of the Risa Star, given to him by Inari the white fox the night he had left Earth. It had saved his life on more than one occasion already and, as one-seventh of what the Cult pursued, was exceptionally valuable. He slid the gauntlet onto his left forearm, the language ring onto his middle finger, and the Shard on its cord around his neck under his shirt. Then he made his way to the command deck.

The ship was already surfacing when he arrived, the grimy water bubbling up the sides of the transparent dome, becoming steadily lighter. Ruth, Sardâr, and Bál were already there, all equipped with their possessions and wrapped in warm clothes.

"Come on, we need to get to the hatch." Ruth led

them across the ship through a network of corridors to the bottom of the metal ladder that marked the only way out. She waited for the rumbling to cease and then climbed up and unscrewed the hatch.

The others followed.

The first sensation that hit Jack was the smell: the acrid stench of a sewer system which seemed to cling to and weigh down the air. The sky was almost devoid of stars, the orange hue of light pollution dissipating into the blackness. They were indeed on a river, the top of the turtle's shell forming an island the size of a round-about on the running water. Either side of the water the city closed in, stretching as far as he could see in both directions: a chaotic multitude of buildings, cranes, warehouses, and street lamps. A few bridges arced over, figures and horse-drawn coaches passing across.

"So where are we heading?" he asked.

"That way," Sardâr whispered, gesturing at the bank on one side where stone steps rose from the waterline.

"But how are we going to—?"

Sardâr dropped into the water and began to swim towards the shore, followed by Ruth and Bál.

"You've got to be joking . . ." Wincing and trying to hold his breath, Jack jumped into the river.

The water was freezing, and it was immediately apparent that it was the origin of the stench. Trying not to imagine what might be swilling around his legs, Jack kicked off the side of the ship and front-crawled as quickly as he could towards the bank. He grasped the steps and pulled himself up.

The other three were wringing out their clothes as much as possible.

"Couldn't we have surfaced closer? Or at least used the gangway?" He gasped, trying to rub some warmth into his arms and chest.

"Too obvious," Sardâr whispered. "We're trying not to attract undue attention from the local people, and that would probably not be best served by a gigantic mechanical turtle surfacing in the middle of their river."

"So which way shall we go?" Ruth asked, shivering.

"This way looks as good as any," Sardâr replied.

Jack followed his gesture indicating the alley from the river into the city. It was grimy, unlit, and he was sure he could see someone slumped against the wall about halfway up. It didn't look particularly good to him. But he had little choice as Sardâr led the way, followed by Bál and Ruth.

They moved onto a wider street, this one with lampposts every few feet. There was no pavement: the damp mud was littered with horse dung and pounded by carriage wheels and feet. The buildings all around were mixed: some limestone and green with erosion; others blackened brick; still more looked older and were gabled with black-and-white-painted wood. Candlelight flickered from some windows, illuminating the dust and grime layered on the glass. A couple of carriages passed, and a few pedestrians were making their way up and down the road.

Sardâr nodded to their right, and they began walking, keeping their heads down as much as possible.

Snow and Water

They passed a few groups of people, in little more than rags, huddled against the wind. A few semiconscious individuals, almost all with nearly empty bottles in hand, slumped in doorways. The four of them attracted some odd looks, certainly not least because they seemed to have just returned from a nocturnal bath.

"We need to get out of the open," Sardâr hissed as they crossed paths with an unashamedly staring man. "We can't do anything right now. We need somewhere to stay tonight and base ourselves."

They passed another alley, with a three-floor gabled building on the corner. Warm light spilled out of the grimy windows, highlighting the uppermost flecks of mud on the street. By the amber glow of the nearest lamppost, Jack could make out the writing on the sign creaking slightly in the breeze:

THE KESTREL'S QUILL
§ FREEHOUSE & INN §

"This should do." Sardâr moved over to the threshold on the corner of the alleyway and, giving it a hefty shunt, entered.

Chapter IV
this is albion

The inside of the inn was true to its exterior. It seemed to have been lit with the fewest possible candles, so that patches of light and shadow waltzed across the dark wood side by side. A few booths and stained tables filled most of the floor space. The only other person visible was a plump, greasy-haired woman in an apron, who eyed them suspiciously from the other side of the bar.

"What'll you be wantin', then?" she demanded in what sounded remarkably like a Cockney accent.

"A room for the night, if you please," Sardâr replied, looking around the dusty room uncertainly.

"Can you pay?"

"Well . . ." Sardâr made a point of checking his pockets, but all four of them knew that, unless alchemy could create coins or notes, none of them carried local currency. The elf smiled apologetically and approached the bar to try to negotiate.

Jack took another look around the room. Some of the planks of the ceiling were missing, and a yellow substance dripped into a small pool beneath. A dark brown insect, far too large for comfort, scuttled from under one booth to another. The rug in front of the bar was so tattered and threadbare that it more resembled roadkill.

"We can stay tonight," Sardâr informed them, returning, "but we're going to need to earn some money in some way."

The woman, presumably the landlady, had disappeared behind the bar and emerged with a candle and a key. "You all look pretty strange folk, but you two colored ones not gettin' your own rooms. My clientele would go mad if they found out."

Ruth appeared to have been shocked into silence. Sardâr grimaced weakly but evidently decided now was not the time to engage in a debate about political correctness.

The landlady led them down a thin corridor opposite the entrance, past several doors, and up a stairwell of creaky wood. She unlocked three adjacent rooms and walked into each to light candles. When she was done, she returned to the top of the stairs. "I'll come back up with some hot water. I'm not cookin' anythin' now, so don't bother askin'. Good night."

"What a charming woman," Bál remarked as the candlelight receded down the stairs.

They deposited all their soaking bags and stripped off a few outer layers of wet clothing. True to her words,

28

the landlady returned a few minutes later with several tin basins of warm, slightly murky water. She lit the fireplace in each of the rooms.

Jack and Ruth ended up in the same room. They slung the wet clothes and sacks over the mantelpiece to dry out and went into Sardâr and Bál's room, where they were doing the same.

"So," Sardâr began, when they were all squashed onto the bed, "not exactly what we'd hoped for, but it will do for now."

Bál looked like he thought this was a grievous understatement. Jack got the impression that he had been looking forward to a return to dry land whilst aboard *The Golden Turtle* but now was none too pleased to find that it was not dry and was more mud than land.

"We'll have to keep cover for a while whilst we find out what we need to. Working to fund our stay here will fit that quite well. Jack, Bál—there's likely to be some industrial work not too far away. Ruth, we can probably find you work as a maid or cook."

"And why can't I just get the same job as the other two?"

"You can try, but I doubt you'd be taken on. From what we've just seen, I don't think social equality figures particularly prominently here . . ."

"What are *you* going to do, then?" Bál asked Sardâr, who was now pacing in front of the fireplace.

"I'll go undercover and try to dig up some leads," Sardâr said. "If the Cult are here, which they almost certainly are, then their arrival won't have gone unnoticed.

There will be some new business or criminal presence they'll be using as a front. Now, most importantly we need to work on disguises." He pulled open his bag and, after rummaging a moment, retrieved the metallic egg he was looking for. He gestured for Bál to stand.

Sardâr held the egg out before Bál and muttered a single syllable. It flashed bright green and floated out of his hand, spinning around the elf and the dwarf to create a matrix of emerald light that blurred their silhouettes. A moment later it returned to the elf's hand, and the light faded.

Jack stood and inspected the two of them. As when he had seen the effects on himself and Lucy, the two people before him were still recognizably Bál and Sardâr. It was just that Bál was significantly taller, almost as tall as Jack, and Sardâr's frame had filled out and his ears rounded. It was less of a transformation than a reflection in a fairground house of mirrors.

"We're going to need some more appropriate clothing," Sardâr continued, regarding his and Bál's stretched garments. The dwarf's had actually ripped up the seam on the side, giving him the appearance of a badly stuffed scarecrow. "I'm sure we can procure some from our delightful landlady tomorrow."

Jack and Ruth bid the other two good night and returned to their room. The pail of water had cooled somewhat now, but they still warmed their feet in it. By the time they were done, the water was distinctly murkier than it had been. With no plumbing in sight, they pushed the container outside the door and forgot about it.

Jack didn't feel much cleaner at all for that brief wash. Thorin Salr, supposedly correlating to a millennium earlier than this world, had provided cleaner facilities. Ruth, however, seemed to be dealing with it fine, so he didn't say anything.

Their clothes had warmed by now. They took turns leaving the room while each changed into dry garments and hung the wet ones on the rail. The choice was between the four-poster bed and a few blankets on the wooden floor. Jack grudgingly chose the latter.

Ruth blew out the candle on the bedside table. There was silence for a few moments.

"Are you missing Lucy?" Ruth asked.

The question caught Jack a little off guard. "Well, yeah . . . I don't think we've ever spent this much time apart before. I really hope she's okay . . ."

"So are you two . . . ?"

It took Jack a moment to realize what she was talking about.

"No! No, definitely not. It was never like that. Her and Alex *maybe*, but no—that would be weird." He thought a moment, at a loss for anything to reciprocate with. "Do you miss anyone? Do you remember anyone from before . . . ?"

"I guess I miss the crew a bit. And no, I don't remember anyone. All I've got from before the amnesia is that tattoo and a dream I keep having."

"Dream?"

"It's not much to go on. It doesn't really make that much sense anyway . . ."

They were both silent for quite a few minutes.

"Good night, then."

"Good night."

An indeterminate amount of time passed. Jack rolled over. He could hear Ruth breathing softly in her sleep a few feet away. The single-pane window projected the flickering orange light from the nearest lamppost directly onto his face. He clambered up off the floor and pulled the ragged curtains shut. But it still wasn't dark. Another light shone behind him.

"Inari!" he hissed, spinning around to see the white fox on top of his sheets, twin tails wavering hypnotically on either side of his triangular head. "We can't talk now. Ruth's in here!"

The fox glanced around and caught sight of the figure in the bed. *"Oh! So are you two . . . ?"*

"No! Well, maybe . . . but it's complicated—"

"Ah, 'it's complicated' . . . the eternal deferral of unrequited love . . ."

Jack glared at the fox, now settling himself down on the floor. As before, he did not so much hear the fox's voice as sense it reverberating inside his head. "I was wondering when you'd next turn up. Not much has happened since we left Thorin Salr."

"I know. I've been watching you."

"You can watch us?" Jack replied, slightly alarmed. "Where is it you live, exactly?"

"Here and there. My essence is anchored in the Shard, but I can come and go in spirit form pretty much wherever I please."

"Does that mean you can go and check up on Alex?"

The fox shook his head. *"Alex is, I assume, in Nexus. I would rather not go there. There's a powerful consciousness in that world from which I would do well to conceal my presence."*

"What, the Emperor? Icarus?"

"No. It's the—" But the fox's voice caught in his throat, making him gag. This had happened before when Inari had tried to tell Jack a little too much about his predicament. *"Something else,"* the fox finally managed, giving up.

Jack sighed and sagged back a bit in his seated position. "Great. Just when I think I've got a grip on what's going on, it all changes again." He paused. "In that case, could you possibly go and keep an eye on Lucy?"

The fox nodded. *"In the Sveta Mountains? That shouldn't be too much trouble."*

Jack considered the fox for a moment. "Inari . . . the letter from Isaac which Sardâr read us . . . it said that you weren't who you say you are . . ."

The fox raised his head slightly, looking at him intently. *"Did it, now? Yes, I met Isaac. The brother of Ruth's adoptive father, wasn't he?"*

"You don't know what happened to him, then? Isaac, I mean."

"I'm afraid I do . . . but that would really be giving the game away . . ."

Jack blinked, and the room was dark, devoid of the shimmering white light that seemed to accompany Inari whenever he appeared. The fox was gone.

Chapter V
the daily grind

Dawn brought a weak light upon Albion. From the upstairs window, Jack could see that the city was feeling the labor pains of a new era. The spires of churches and cathedrals jostled with smog-belching funnels and rattling cranes. Fragile cobbled streets lined with gabled houses were now intersected by wide, mud-swept roads that acted like arteries for carriages and carts. In contrast to the old sculpted wood and stone, factories sat like blackened brick behemoths, engorging workers and spewing out mechanically produced goods. Yet beyond the haze encircling the buildings, Jack could just about make out pale green hills on the horizon.

It didn't take long for Jack and Bál, having raided the storerooms of the inn for appropriate clothing, to find work. They walked a couple of streets up from The Kestrel's Quill to discover a foreman's assistant, who had set up a makeshift desk on the side of the road and was signing men up for factory work.

Jack was unsurprised to see Bál unsure on his feet, having grown to human height overnight; his clumsiness drew a few odd looks from fellow applicants and a snide remark from the foreman's assistant. Having had their names taken down—a necessity, it seemed, because many of the fellow men were illiterate—the two of them joined the lumbering march across the town to the factory building.

Ruth, meanwhile, had found a job through the landlady, whose niece worked as a maid in an aristocrat's city household only a few hundred feet from the inn. Apparently consulting a mental address book, the landlady had pointed Ruth in the direction of a woman she knew would hire "coloreds."

Upon her meek arrival at the servants' entrance, Ruth discovered the lady of the house's ward was herself not white. The so-called house was more of a manor: an impressive whitish-grey building with wide columns not unlike a temple's. It clearly belonged to a wealthy district entirely apart from The Kestrel's Quill quarter and the rest of the city.

Sardâr had left before the others had awoken, leaving only a note in the most ambiguous terms explaining that he was going on a fact-finding mission and would see them that evening. Jack suspected he didn't want the landlady, with her clientele apparently fervently committed to bigotry, to have too much of an idea what he was up to.

At school, Jack had enjoyed learning about the industrial revolution, but nothing could have prepared him for this factory. The dark-bricked cuboid squatted by the riverside, encircled by a rusting cast-iron fence and a collection of ramshackle outhouses. Chimneys rose from its apex like dark spires, belching smoke into the air to be sifted over the rooftops by the wind. A thick crowd of men poured over the cobbles into the forecourt, foremen assigning them through various stable-like doors. Jack and Bál joined the mob, trying not to trip and be engulfed by the many boots marching relentlessly onwards as if belonging to some kind of gigantic millipede. They were swept beneath the sign on the gate—Goodwin Construction Ltd.—and, directed by a man on a soapbox, dragged off in a slipstream through one of the dim entrances.

The first thing that hit them was the noise: the clanging and grinding of machinery refracting off the walls and floor. The room was cavernous, the upper half a matrix of leather pulleys and metal piping. Two of the chimneys extended through the chamber like trunks, their bases, if not the heat emanating from them, obscured by the aisles of interconnected devices. Jack breathed in and spluttered—the air was pummelled with gases and particles thicker than oxygen.

He glanced at Bál. The dwarf's eyes were wide in shock and possibly terror, much more so than they had been in the midst of battle. Jack had to remind himself that the dwarf could never have conceived anything like this, his own kingdom being almost a millennium away from this kind of economic progress.

Though the crowd had slimmed, they were still carried with considerable force past the aisles. Perhaps hundreds of men were already here, operating the machinery, stoking the chimneys, and shifting a plethora of metal components about. They all, without exception, looked exhausted and ill. Their backs were hunched with strain, and grease and dirt matted their clothes, hair, and skin. Jack noticed many with missing limbs and some with open wounds that still seemed to be bleeding. Something knocked into his thigh, and he looked down to see a child, no older than seven or eight, bow his head in apology and scuttle away, hugging a hefty iron disc to his chest.

Somehow, Jack and Bál found themselves in front of a line of consoles with a group of other men. Apparently aware of the next step, the others stepped up and began busying themselves with the operation. Jack and Bál hung back.

"What do we do?" the dwarf roared at him over the din.

"I don't know," Jack shouted back, shrugging. The contraption before them looked ancient and seeped oil.

He watched the man next to him take a metal rod the length of a cricket bat from a bundle on the left and clamp it in place. With a switch, the man turned on a spinning blade, which made contact with the rod with a grinding shriek. Hot ribbons of metal and sparks cascaded off. After a couple of minutes, the blade was released and stopped spinning. The man dropped the rod, now thinner along one-third of its length, into a tin barrel to the right and took up the next one.

Jack stepped up to his machine and, showing Bál how to do it, completed his first rod. It wasn't particularly even, and he had to apply quite a lot of force to keep the blade in place for two minutes.

Wiping the sweat from his brow, he dropped the rod into the barrel and turned to the man he'd watched. "What are we making?"

The man looked up with red-rimmed eyes, shrugged, and returned to his task.

The working day was much longer than either of them had thought possible. Once light began to fade from the massive grime-encrusted window above them, gas lamps were lit at every few workstations. The labor quickly became mind-numbingly dull and then actively painful. The workers could not sit down and so had to hunch over the consoles, shifting their weight to keep both feet working. The factory floor was stiflingly hot, and Jack suffered several coughing fits when the smoke-heavy air became too much. Oil quickly ingrained their clothes and arms, and their muscles ached from applying pressure to the spinning blade.

Foremen prowled between the aisles all day, batons in hand, clearly searching for anyone who appeared to be slacking. Just as at school, Jack could sense the others around him working particularly efficiently whenever they were being watched. But, at school, relaxing too long hadn't earned anyone a beating. He witnessed an elderly man in the next aisle being dragged out under the arms, a bruise blossoming on his temple.

Jack could feel Bál shifting next to him, instinctively reaching for the axe that was usually by his side. Jack placed a warning hand on the dwarf's arm. He was as disgusted as Bál, but they were under strict instructions from Sardâr not to draw attention to themselves. He had to resist the urge to exact quick and undetectable alchemical revenge on the guilty foreman.

Finally, once all sense of time had been drained from the two of them, Jack became aware that the mechanical noises were quieting. The men finished their tasks and stepped away from the machines, easing their muscles. Jack and Bál did the same and joined the slow trail of dirty bodies trudging out of the factory. Small pouches of coins, incredibly light, were handed to each upon their exit from the building.

"Not great pay, is it?" a boy next to Jack commented, rattling the bag.

"Nope," Jack croaked, his voice hoarse from thirst.

"Oh, well. I guess it'll buy dinner."

Jack couldn't even muster the energy to agree as the boy turned left out of the forecourt and disappeared into the crowd.

Lucy could see them at least half an hour before they reached the camp: three insubstantial mounds, almost like dark igloos. She had first thought they had been small tents, until they drew close enough for her to make out the shuffling movements and the glint of reptilian eyes reflecting the snow.

Their journey across the plain was arduous, and it took much longer than they'd expected. The snow was piled thicker on the flatlands, and in places they found themselves trudging through freezing powder. The wind cut harder the farther they ventured into the open, sheets of daggers sliding into any exposed flesh and pounding it deep crimson. Lucy's gut, already uncomfortable, was wrenched with hunger when they halted, shivering, several feet before the goblin trio.

"Welcome," the central goblin called in a Slavic-like accent, her hoarse voice barely audible over the wind. "We do not receive many visitors here." She was immensely old, her greyish-green scaly skin cracked into wrinkles around her eyes and mouth. What Lucy had taken to be obesity at a distance was actually a cocoon of matted furs and hides wrapped around her so as to only leave her face and gloved hands visible. The two either side, both male, were taller but more lightly wrapped, and both carried spears from which shreds of cloth fluttered.

"We mean you no harm." Hakim laid down his staff. "We have come in search of an alchemical artifact and to deliver a message to you. Perhaps there is somewhere we can talk?"

The goblin matriarch nodded and turned, shuffling through the snow into the midst of the campsite. Lucy, Vince, Adâ, and Hakim followed, the two goblin guards closing ranks behind them.

The campsite seemed to have been constructed to provide maximum wind resistance for those moving about within: tents assembled in concentric circles with minimal gaps between them. As they passed through the aisle between two banks of canvases, the resident goblins clambered out onto thresholds to watch them intently.

Lucy felt slightly uneasy. The goblins she had met before had been quite happy to mix with elves. They had even recognized her and Jack as humans through their alchemical disguises, but to expect the same of these would be like assuming there were no racist humans. If this community was as segregated from the outer world as it seemed, they might not react well to alien visitors.

At the center of the campsite stood the tallest tent, a domed structure decorated with tribal patterns and weighted with snow. The goblin matriarch disappeared beneath the awning, and the travelers followed her.

The interior was significantly warmer. It was lit by a circle of candles set in the center of the floor, a few flickering out from their movement as they stooped to maneuver into seated positions. Some sort of stylized map was cut into the material of the floor between the candles, depicting mountains, rivers, and several other locales. What appeared to be the matriarch's living space was on the opposite side of the entrance: a nest of furs, thick hides, and rugs, into which she now settled herself.

The candlelight did little to penetrate the darkness encircling the group of travelers. The matriarch retrieved a slender wooden stick and proceeded to relight some of the candles. The only other illumination was the humming glow of four language rings as the goblin began to speak.

"I believe I already know what you seek. The Fifth Shard of the Risa Star, long since entrusted to my tribe to protect. It is our most holy relic. We will not yield it lightly." She completed the circle and, raising the wand to her lips, blew out the flame.

"We do not seek it lightly," Hakim responded. "We are Apollonians: we represent an organization which aims to reunite the Risa Star to defend our worlds against the Darkness."

The matriarch fixed him with her gaze, piercing despite her age. "You are either familiar with our legends or have similar ones of your own. We have guarded the Shard against the Darkness far longer than your organization has sought it. Even if it is to be used for good, why should we give it up to you?"

"That's the message we've come to deliver," Vince cut in. "There's another organization, the Cult of Dionysus—our mirror image, if you like—that wants to obtain the Shards to create a superweapon. If they succeed, Darkness will pour into our universe like never before."

"And you believe this Cult is here, in the Sveta Mountains?"

"We know it. Or they're at least on their way. We mean no disrespect"—he eyed the guards, who had followed them inside with their spears—"but you've never faced anything like them before. Particularly not the two archbishops who've specifically been dispatched to extract the Shard from you."

The matriarch regarded him imperiously. "We are not savages, human. We know how to defend ourselves and that which we love."

"Of course, we know," Adâ replied, bowing her head slightly, "but we still think our expertise would not go amiss. How might we convince you of our need to take the Shard?"

"The high priest is currently praying at the Shard's resting place at the Cave of Lights. You may converse with him on such matters when he returns. Until then"— the matriarch stood—"we will provide for you."

The guests got to their feet and bowed their heads, understanding themselves to be dismissed.

The guards led them out of the tent and into the biting gale. A small crowd had accumulated outside the matriarch's quarters, evidently curious about the visitors.

One of the guards raised his spear and called over the wind, "These travelers are our guests until the high priest returns from prayer. Who amongst you will share your home to give them keep?"

The response wasn't exactly stirring. There were mutterings, and those in the front shrunk backwards as if they would be picked on just for being most visible. The guards scanned the group for a few moments. Then, finally, a solitary, thickly wrapped hand rose.

"Many thanks, Maht. The matriarch will consider you kindly."

The crowd dispersed. The goblin who had volunteered was left looking slightly forlorn and more than a little intimidated, and the four tall strangers approached her. She was slight, even though enshrined in layers of clothing, with wispy dark hair that was partially beaded. She coughed a little whilst beckoning them to follow her.

Maht led the four into one of the alleyways, moving round the circle of tents until they had lost sight of the entrance. She halted outside one of the smaller tents and hoisted the flap, ushered them inside, and folded it shut behind them.

Maht's dwelling was far less grand than the matriarch's. It seemed to be a general practice that tents were lit by a circle of candles in the center of the floor, though this one was significantly smaller. Furs were piled to the left of the entrance, where a small goblin girl was curled up asleep. The goblin's few possessions—a collection of pots, bundles of long candles, and sealed jars that seemed to make up some kind of larder—were stacked around the rest of the room.

Maht busied herself rearranging the furs to create as much additional sleeping space as possible. "Please, make yourselves comfortable. Would you like a drink? Or something to eat?"

Lucy nodded vigorously, and the other three seconded, though rather more politely.

As they settled themselves upon the furs and peeled off layers of soaked clothing, the goblin scooped some snow in a tin and began to warm it over the candles. She rummaged through a few pots and handed them each a sphere the size of a baseball.

Lucy sniffed it and bit into it hesitantly. It tasted a little like Christmas stuffing but with stronger spices.

"What is this?"

Maht looked around, surprised and slightly wary. "It's herb bread, mixed with salted meat. We make it in the summer months and store it for the winter."

"It's good," Lucy replied, keen to make her last question seem less indignant. And it *was* good and surprisingly filling. She could feel the tension in her stomach easing with every mouthful.

The others were finishing theirs with relish. Maht decanted the hot water into four metal cups and passed one to each of them. Lucy tasted it; it seemed to be some kind of thick broth.

Vince, Adâ, and Hakim had piled their wet clothes next to the circle of candles. Lucy did the same and tried to find a comfortable position on the furs. Considering they were only inches from snow, it was considerably warm in here. She had been camping as a child, and this wasn't so different at all.

"Thanks for letting us stay," Vince said as the goblin woman settled herself next to her child.

Maht smiled slightly, before closing her eyes and pulling her daughter a little closer.

The Daily Grind

Chapter VI
ə dəy off

That week was probably the longest in Jack's life. It didn't take him long to decide there were places he'd much rather be than Albion. He and Lucy hadn't been particularly impressed at being catapulted from Earth into a war zone, but at least in Thorin Salr there had been a clear plan and sense of progress: rescue Sardâr; be trained in combat and alchemy; fend off a Cult insurgency; forge a peace deal with the goblins. In Albion, they seemed to be accomplishing nothing, and there was no end in sight.

The workweek was six days long, and it seemed only the last vestiges of preindustrial tradition kept the factory owners from illegalizing weekends. Factory days were even longer than Jack and Bál's first had been. Having to rise before dawn, and without a chance for lunch, they were barely able to stand by the time the bell tolled for them to finish. The few hours of sleep they scraped at night were hardly sufficient to keep them awake and alert throughout the following day.

In his time at the factory, Jack witnessed the brutality he had read about in school. There were four incidences of major accidents on the floor, in which limbs were mangled or sheared off by machinery. He tried not to look when the injured men were escorted out, leaving a thin trail of blood along their exit route, but in some cases he could not help himself. One of these was so grotesque that he had to stop working in order to bend over and retch. The threat of a nearby foreman's baton, however, returned him to his task.

Once, towards the end of the week, a miniature strike was started: a group of men in the next aisle put down their tools and linked arms, claiming they would not work any longer until they were paid enough to feed their families. One began passing round pamphlets, authored by an apparently notorious political figure, entitled "The Brutal Power of Capital and How We Can Break It." The culprits were swiftly dealt with. The strikers were beaten and told that they would be paid nothing if they did not work, and the foreman began randomly searching workers for the treasonous pamphlet. More than one was clubbed until his skull bled and he had to be dragged outside.

Ruth's work, whilst less harrowing, was barely less arduous. She had arrived on her first day and been immediately co-opted into the scrubbing of the kitchen floor. The woman in charge of the domestic duties, Matron Flint, ran the household with military precision and efficiency. Tasks were allocated in rotation, for which a comprehensive credit system had been devised. Those women and girls who did not fulfill their daily credit quota, whether because of fatigue or laziness, did not have to wait long to feel the back of Matron Flint's hand.

On her first day, Ruth had found herself, amongst other duties, washing laundry, brushing the stairs, laying the table for supper, shining the silverware, and dusting the banisters. Though she glimpsed a few visitors to the house, at no point did she see its mistress, her employer.

With the joint earnings of the three of them and shared rooms, they just managed to afford their accommodation cost and two meals a day, with a little left over. The Kestrel's Quill was gratifyingly cheap, though hardly a monument to culinary achievement. Jack, seeing someone else order a meat dish, settled on a broth which, while watery and insubstantial, was at least hot. Bál seemed rather offended by the lack of roasted hog or whatever he had come to expect back in the halls of his homeland. Ruth, as a vegetarian, had to be contented with a plate of soggy potatoes, carrots, and greens.

Jack wouldn't have described weekends at home as *good*, necessarily, but they provided a welcome relief to the dirge of schooltime. By the end of the sixth day in the factory, he looked forward to a break more than he ever had in his life. He and Bál staggered back to the inn, ingested their dinner, and made their way instantly to bed, comforted by the prospect of a full night's sleep.

He awoke late the next morning. Patches of light swivelled over the floor and his blankets, filtered through grimy glass and the thin curtains. Ruth apparently was already up, her bed left unmade. Jack clambered to his knees and shuffled over to the basin of water, splashing his face. His eyes were almost glued shut with the various amalgamated substances they had inherited from the factory and inn. Now able to see a little better, he caught his reflection in the mirror. Upon reverting to human form from his elf disguise, his body had not lost all its new muscularity, the product of three weeks of combat training. But now he looked gaunt, his ribs protruding unpleasantly from his torso. Machine oil streaked his arms, and there was a noticeable line where his shirt-sleeves had been rolled up.

"No offence, but you haven't got that much to be vain about at the moment." Ruth was leaning in the now open doorway.

Sheepishly, he grabbed his shirt and pulled it over his filthy body.

The girl laughed a little, apologetically. "So what do you want to do today, then?"

Doing something other than resting with his day off hadn't occurred to him. "I don't know. What did you have in mind?"

"We could go exploring."

"Okay." Jack was uncertain there was much to explore in this city, but it was worth a go if it allowed him to spend some time with Ruth. "What about Bál?"

"I tried to ask him, but he's fast asleep."

"And still no sign of Sardâr?"

The girl shook her head. They hadn't seen the elf once since their first night at The Kestrel's Quill. Bál had insisted that Sardâr had arrived late and departed early each day from the other bedroom, but this didn't really assuage the discomfort in Jack's gut. The last time the elf had gone on a solitary expedition, he had fallen into a Cultist trap and endured a period of imprisonment guarded by a powerful demon. Jack didn't know at what point they should start to worry.

"Come on, let's get going. It's past midday." Ruth led the way.

Jack followed her out of the room. Shutting the door, he glanced back up the corridor, silently glad Bál would not be accompanying them.

The two of them spent the day, or what remained of it, wandering around Albion. There was not, they agreed, much that they weren't already aware of: a river, the city's trading hub; pockets of rich houses amongst the general throng of impoverished ones; cluttered residential streets; factories; and a central commercial sector. Jack thought the buildings in this last area were, if not attractive, certainly impressive. The roads here were wider and cleaner, divided into a rational plan of white stone buildings with colonnades and steps comprising what seemed to be a variety of business headquarters, stock markets, art galleries, and upmarket theatres.

Domes of cathedrals and music halls alike rose out of the smog, redeeming slightly the idea that the city hadn't seemed entirely lost to purely economic pursuits. They found a fountain in the middle of a relatively quiet square which they settled themselves on, clutching the luxury of lunch thanks to the additional wages they had accumulated over the week.

Jack yawned loudly. Ruth giggled.

"What? I'm tired. Aren't you?"

"Yeah, I'm shattered but clearly not that much!"

The fountain bubbled behind them, misting on their backs. It was a refreshing change to the dry heat of the factory.

They were silent for a while, content to watch the people pass and a pair of birds winging their way about the square.

"Missing home yet?" Ruth asked eventually.

Jack had to think about it. He missed Lucy, certainly, and, though he'd not known them long at all, Adâ and Hakim. He missed Alex, though that worry now went back so far that it had become part of his consciousness; his absence wasn't a fresh wound in the same way that Lucy's was.

He began slowly. "I think home's probably more about people than a place. I don't miss my orphanage or my town or even my *planet*, but I miss Lucy and Alex and all the rest of them . . ."

"You and Alex were close, then?"

"Yeah, we were. Best mates, I guess, for a long time." He exhaled, gazing across the square to where a couple of children were playing. "Did you know him?"

"Yeah, I knew Alex." Ruth smiled distantly and, for some reason, Jack suddenly felt a little sick.

"Were you two . . . ?"

It took Ruth a moment to realize what he meant, but then her smile faded into disbelief. "No! No, not at all. We just got on well. I can see why you liked him. Actually, I've got my suspicions about . . ." She trailed off.

"What?"

"No," she corrected herself, "don't worry."

There was a pause, in which Jack began to tear up his lunch wrappings.

Ruth leant a little closer and hugged him lightly around the waist. The brush of her arm on his stomach sent shivers up to his neck. "Don't worry. I'm sure he's doing okay."

the black rose

Chapter VII
tales

They arrived back at The Kestrel's Quill just as the sun was beginning to set. This time on a Sunday was apparently when everyone came to drink: the inn was packed, mostly with men who seemed, by their clothing, to hold similar jobs to Jack and Bál. Jack scanned the crowd, but he couldn't see Bál or Sardâr amongst them.

"We've still got some spare change, haven't we?" Ruth asked.

"Yeah, I think so," Jack replied, producing a few coins from his pocket.

"Come on. Let's get a drink." Ruth somehow slid her way through the crowd to the bar and called a few words to the landlady over the din. Coins were handed over, and she shortly returned with two flagons of frothy amber liquid.

"What is this?" Jack asked, sniffing warily.

"Not sure. I couldn't make out what she was saying. It tastes alright, though."

Jack tried it. It was bitter and not particularly pleasant, but he didn't want to make a fuss in front of Ruth, so he swallowed it in what he hoped was a nonchalant way. As soon as her back was turned, he spat as subtly as possible onto the floor, trying to clear the taste.

They deliberated, and then squeezed into seats at a nearby table. Ruth was drinking her pint at a considerable pace, and he felt obliged to keep up with her. It fizzled up his nostrils, and he had to suppress a splutter. The more he drank, the less he liked what he was drinking. Moreover, he felt himself becoming increasingly light-headed the further the froth reached down the inside of the flagon. The liquid made him feel uncomfortably full, too, as if his insides were a churning barrel. But Ruth seemed completely unaffected, so he soldiered on as best he could.

The people at the table quieted slightly, apparently all listening to a man in the center.

"There's rumors of strange folk around. Men in black cloaks who're runnin' a big business operation. Somethin' to do with the Goodwin factory. And a woman, a temptress, who comes and goes on the cold wind and beguiles men—"

"Ruth, I'm not feeling so good," Jack said.

"You're not livin' in the country anymore, Tommy," another across the table called. "This is Albion. There's no room for your farmer's fairy stories 'ere."

56

"Ruth, I'm really not feeling great."

"Where were these men seen?" Ruth asked the first man, ignoring the interrupters.

But before she could get a reply, Jack had vomited onto the floor next to her.

The table erupted into jeers. Jack's head was spinning. He was aware of being pulled away from the table and guided out of the barroom and up the stairs. Ruth kicked open the door to their room and supported him onto the bed. He couldn't find the willpower to sit up straight. In his periphery, he saw Ruth tossing the murky contents of the basin out the window before positioning it under his dripping mouth.

For a few moments, Ruth was silent whilst Jack spat a little more into the basin. Then she broke into a laugh. "You didn't even manage one pint!"

"Yeah, I know," Jack spluttered. He felt foolish and angry with himself for having put on this performance in front of Ruth, of all people.

"Well, I suppose you must've lost quite a lot of body weight this week . . . And we haven't been eating properly . . ."

"Yeah, let's go with that," Jack replied, appreciative of her efforts to save some of his pride. He was more thankful still when Ruth came to sit next to him on the bed and placed an arm around him. "Do you think that guy knows anything useful about the Cult?"

"I don't know, but we can go back and ask him in a bit. Maybe . . ."

Jack was aware of the door opening and someone

stepping inside. He and Ruth looked up, surprised.

In the doorway stood a sailor or, rather, the exact caricature of a sailor, with a heavily woven jumper, a thick raincoat and boots, a flat cap, and even a pipe, which protruded from his bearded face.

"Who are you?" Ruth demanded.

"For Davy Jones's sake, it's me," the figure replied, fumbling with the hat and beard. A moment later, Sardâr's face emerged. "I've clearly got a little *too* into character." His gaze moved to Jack, who was feebly crouched on the bed. He grunted in annoyance. "I've spent a week undercover in the presence of some of the slyest and sharpest men I've ever met, and meanwhile you've been drinking yourselves into a stupor! Come on, both of you, next door. We've got a lot to talk about."

There was, it seemed, little work to be done in the goblin camp during the long haul of the winter season. With all the provisions collected and stored during the summer and autumn, the goblins were mainly preoccupied with keeping warm and vigilantly protecting their home. From slender wooden towers raised sporadically among tents, sentries held watch every night, always returning chilled to the core by the piercing wind.

For the most extreme climate Lucy had ever found herself in, the time they were spending there was frustratingly dull. She and varying combinations of the other Apollonians took excursions around the encampment, but, with little to occupy their attention other than what there was to see in Maht's tent, she always returned fairly soon afterwards. The matriarch, it seemed, dwelt in almost continual solitude, enshrined within her fur nest, pondering her ring of candles.

The one occupation Lucy found was when Maht's daughter, Doch, was awake. Appearing only five or six years old, she had wide blue eyes and an even wider mouth. Not remotely intimidated by the discovery that she now shared her home with four strangers, she had made a point of introducing herself to each of them. She had fixed Lucy with an expansive stare before announcing phonetically: "My name's Doch. What's yours?"

"Hi. I'm Lucy. Doch—that's a funny name."

"No, you've got a funny name. Loo-see."

Wandering around the encampment, Lucy became aware of a difference in Maht's household. Every other family she saw had either a father or an elder son, mostly in the service of the guards. During the winter months not having a man around probably didn't matter much, she supposed, but Maht must have had a hard time during the sowing and harvesting seasons.

She asked the goblin about it one evening. "Doch's father . . . What happened to him?"

Maht was sewing at this point. She pushed the needle through the fabric and took her time pulling the thread to its full length. "He left. It's not usual for the men here to leave, but that didn't stop him. He went to seek his fate elsewhere and left her . . . and me."

Lucy felt a rush of affection for the woman. "Have

you ever thought of finding someone else?" The question sounded stunted, even cruel.

Maht looked up from her sewing and smiled. "The women of my tribe are famously strong. We do not need men to command our lives. I can raise Doch by myself. The men can come and go, but we remain."

As the affection mingled with pride, Lucy returned the smile.

Later, when the goblins were asleep, the group of Apollonians were crouched around the circle of candles. There had been little to talk about, so they had said little. Now, with no prospect of developments ahead of them, Lucy decided to find out more about their situation. "So who are the Cultists we're up against this time? Phaedra and Paethon?"

To Lucy's slight surprise, it was not Hakim, the fountain of knowledge, but Vince who answered. "They're twins. Girl and boy."

"How do you know about them?"

Vince took a hefty swig from the wooden cup clutched in his fingers and put it to one side, rubbing his hands in front of the flames. "They're the reason I got involved with the Apollonians in the first place. My elder sister and I grew up on a council estate in Scotland, and she sometimes had to go away for days at a time. Then, one time, she disappeared."

"She didn't come back?"

Vince's expression tautened. "Oh, she came back. She came back in a shoe box. That's when I met Isaac. He came and explained what had happened. She'd been on a humanitarian aid mission to a world ravaged by the Cult when they mounted a second attack. Those two—Phadrea and Paethon—were leading it, and they set fire to the land. My sister was burnt alive."

He let out a long, low breath, shadows of candle flames flickering across his face. "They murdered her because she was trying to help the people they wanted to conquer. She did nothing to them. That's why I'm here, on this particular mission. I've wanted the chance to come face-to-face with them ever since I found out what they did. I want to make them pay." Vince finished, his eyes glazed over.

Adâ and Hakim looked despondent. Lucy grimaced, wishing she hadn't asked.

the black rose

Chapter VIII
lady osborne

"I've *finally* got some idea of what's going on," Sardâr said. He had taken to his usual pacing before the fireplace, his shadow twisting in and out over the uneven wooden floor. The flickering light of a street lamp shone through the window. The other three Apollonians were crowded onto the bed, Bál still in his nightclothes.

"So where've you been this week?" Ruth asked.

"Undercover. I've been a courier, a clerk, a porter, a pickpocket, a debt collector, a sailor—and you have *no* idea how much criminal activity is going on under the surface of this city. I've chased up several leads which have turned out to be parts of completely separate undertakings, not relevant to the Cult at all, and I've been very tempted to intervene. Robberies, smuggling, fraud, blackmail, embezzlement—but we're here for a purpose, so I've let things lie. And now I think I've got enough evidence to give us an idea of how things stand."

He stopped pacing, staring intently at the three of them. The reflection of flames from the fireplace shimmered across the left side of his face.

"As it turns out, by apparent chance, your workplaces have been linked with this. The prime object of my investigations"—he turned to Ruth—"has been your employer, Lady Osborne. She is a new presence in the city, who is apparently married to a very successful businessman. She has been in contact with several of the major manufacturing firms, one of which is"—he now turned to Jack and Bál—"your employer, Mister Goodwin of Goodwin Construction Limited—who, I might add, would fit very comfortably into the criminal underworld if he didn't have a family reputation to safeguard."

"Well, I'm not surprised," Bál snorted, "given the way he treats his workforce."

Jack grimaced, all too aware that his one day off was swiftly drawing to a close.

"So you think this woman—*my boss*—is somehow connected to the Cult?" Ruth said.

"Yes, the timing of her arrival works out alongside the Cult's. Lady Osborne, whether or not that is her real name, seems to be overseeing the construction of something. What it is, exactly, I do not know. No one I have spoken to, even when their tongue has been loosened by a few drinks, could tell me anything about it. All I know, thanks to a cooperative dockside clerk I happened to

come across, is that its eventual destination is upriver."
He fell silent.

The three on the bed exchanged looks. Jack was struck suddenly by how dirty they all were, having spent over a week in a smog-soaked city without washing properly. He thought he and Bál had looked bad, but Sardâr looked as if he'd been dragged through the countryside during an autumn thunderstorm. He had exchanged his sailor garments for some more generic ones, but these were barely cleaner.

"So I presume you want me to find out more, then?" Ruth prompted him.

"Yes. We have an advantage in that Lady Osborne has no idea who you really are, so you could be an ideal spy in the household. Be on the lookout for anything out of the ordinary—well, out of the ordinary for Albion—and report back. I think we can safely assume the Cult hasn't got its hands on the Third Shard yet; otherwise they wouldn't be undercover. The top priority at the moment is to find out what is being made and where they're planning to take it. That might give a clue as to where the Shard is."

Jack, Bál, and Ruth nodded. Despite the situation in which they and Sardâr found themselves increasingly submerged, Jack smirked. They had a direction and a purpose again.

Not so far away, across the misty streets in which

drunkards stumbled, gangs loitered, and the homeless huddled, the Osborne household was dark except for one room. Although the curtains facing the street below were pulled shut, hints of orange light sifted outwards, beckoning attention to the plotting within.

Frost gripped the furnishings. Nimue reclined on her throne of ice, her twelve companions standing in a semicircle before her. Moments earlier, they might have formed a tableau of Albion society, a cross section of the class strata from newly inherited earl to forgettable workhouse resident. Now, however, like their mistress's, their parochial garb had faded into the swishing of twelve hooded black cloaks. Behind Nimue's seat stood the mirror, the dark-skinned girl still frozen in its depths.

"All the components are ready, then?"

"All of them, madam. They have been sourced from different firms so as to not arouse suspicion, and all have had the appropriate alchemical adjustments."

"Excellent. Then we shall begin assembling them this very night. Bring them to the cellar beneath this house. It links to a subterranean canal which emerges onto the river. We

Lady Osborne

will then make our move tomorrow night."

The twelve figures nodded in unison.

"And what is our plan once we reach the forest?" one inquired, but Nimue held a finger to her mouth. She turned her head towards the door and flicked her palm. The lock clicked and the wooden frame sprang open, a middle-aged woman in servant clothes tumbling onto the carpet. She pulled herself up, eyes wide with fright, scanning the ice, the mirror, and the collection of dark figures before her.

Her mouth opened in a scream but, after another flick of Nimue's palm, nothing emerged but a frost-clouded breath. The door slammed behind her, and the lock clicked. The maid was hoisted off the floor by her throat and flung across the room, dropped hard before the mistress's throne.

"Listening in, were we?" Nimue whispered, her jaw set in a cold smirk. "Now that wasn't very polite, was it? I don't expect a provincial type like yourself to understand the magnitude of what we are attempting, but even so, whispers might find their way to the wrong ears . . ."

The maid's gaze was fixed on Nimue, but she became aware of something shifting behind her. The shadows thrown by the lamplight were congealing, rising off the floor and twisting upwards. Nimue's smirk broke into a tinkling laugh as the shadow reared and leapt. The maid's scream was never heard.

Jack, Bál, and Ruth returned to work the following morning unenthusiastic but energized. Jack still found the duration, fatigue, and hot conditions of the factory work nearly unbearable, but at least he knew their group would've progressed closer to their goal by the time he returned to The Kestrel's Quill. Now that he knew of his employer's association with Lady Osborne, the metal poles he and the other men were shaping intrigued him. Could these have some part in the Cult's plan, whatever it was? He saw an opportunity to delve a little deeper when he found himself on a workstation next to the uncommonly amicable boy he had exchanged a few words with on the first day. The boy evidently recognized him too because he smiled—highly unusual in the factory environment.

"How'd your pay stretch the other day, then?" the boy asked in the thick Cockney accent Jack had become used to over the last week.

"Not very far at all." Jack laughed. "But I managed to get drunk off it last night." He didn't try too hard to keep the boasting edge out of his voice.

"Well, that's something at least. I saved up for a Sunday roast—definitely worth it." The boy grinned. "I'm Dannie, by the way."

"Jack." They shook hands. "You don't have any idea what we're making, do you?"

"None at all." Dannie shook his head, glancing at the contraption before him in bewilderment. "Apparently

Lady Osborne

this Goodwin fellow's a nasty piece of work though. Forbids any trade union membership among his employees, owns a big stake in the workhouses, and has his fingers in some very rotten pies from what I've heard . . ."

Ruth, meanwhile, had thought through her plan on the way to work. She needed an excuse to get into the upstairs drawing room, where Lady Osborne met all her associates and likely kept her documents. She found her alibi when Matron Flint fervently allocated to her the dusting on the first floor. Ruth made sure to do a particularly thorough job around the doorway of the drawing room until, as soon as no one was around, she twisted the handle and slipped inside.

Even by the standards she had become used to in this house, the room was ridiculously decorated. Seemingly every surface rippled with some kind of design in motion: an erratic diamond-patterned carpet, fleur-de-lis-encrusted wallpaper, floral cushions and upholstery, lamps carved and smelted in the shape of forest beasts, and an absurdly decorous mahogany table on the opposite wall. A dank portrait of a stout old man hung on the wall behind the desk. The panels of dusty light falling from the windows lent the contemporary room the impression of being already very outdated.

Ruth made sure no one was about and then shuffled quickly over to the desk. A few papers were scattered over its surface. She riffled through them—bills, invoices, a couple of letters—nothing substantial in the way of evidence. She tried one of the hefty drawers, but it was stuck. She tried again, gripping the handle through her apron, but nothing. She glanced around for something to pick the lock with and stopped dead.

A girl was sitting on one of the sofas opposite her, so embalmed in beauty products that Ruth had initially taken her to be part of the ludicrously patterned furniture. But what was more unsettling was that the girl didn't seem to have registered Ruth's arrival at all. She was staring into the middle distance, porcelain face entirely blank of expression. In fact, she could have been a statue—her hands were folded in her lap in a formal fashion, and she didn't even appear to be breathing.

Ruth allowed herself to exhale and released the edge of the desk, which she had instinctively gripped. She shook her head, slowly walking around the desk and the obstacle course of furniture to stand in front of the girl, who still didn't react. Ruth stooped and waved inches in front of her face. Nothing.

"Are you alright?" she said loudly, touching the side of the girl's head.

Ruth immediately cried out and pulled away. The girl was evaporating before her eyes, skin and cloth vanishing. Within seconds there was nothing to suggest the girl had ever been there.

There was a crackling sound behind her.

Heart pounding, Ruth spun around and staggered back, almost collapsing over a footstool. The grubby painting had disappeared. In its place, a full-length mirror hung, its surface perfectly smooth and unscratched. Frost clouded the insides, but through the mist Ruth could clearly see the figure of the porcelain girl hanging above the ground, expressionless face staring directly at her.

Chapter IX
dark alchemy

Alex screamed as the flames scorched his flesh, incin-
erating layers of skin. He almost passed out, and, in his
struggle to remain conscious, he felt suddenly adrift. He
could see everything that had happened since his arrival.

Despite the Emperor's apparently magnanimous
gesture to release him from prison, not much had really
changed. He was no longer chained, but he had been
confined to the Cathedral and allocated a room somewhere high in one of the towers. It was excessively
simple: circular, the floor space the size of an elevator
shaft, with only a small bed and an alchemically barred
window. Constructed entirely of stone, it was freezing,
but at least he could now use alchemy. Most of his energies were spent keeping a fire burning.

He had considered trying to escape, but his ventures
to the building's outer doors confirmed that black-

cloaked Cultists guarded every entrance. His only view beyond the Cathedral was his small window, and that was hardly comforting: a sprawl of lights from clustered houses and mighty skyscrapers; beyond that, churning ocean, sporadically illuminated by crunching lightning.

By day, his overwhelming emotions were of boredom and depression, but by night he found himself on the edge of a sea of fear. He knew of the unspeakable acts that went on in Nexus, directed at those captured in invasions or dissenters from the autocratic government and religion. He was woken from uneasy sleep by screams rising out of the darkness, wailing and begging for relief, for the torment to end by any way possible.

The Emperor had visited him several days after their talk in the throne room. Alex initially had reacted with incredulity, then with angered stubbornness, at his suggestion. "You want to teach me Dark alchemy? Are you crazy?"

The Emperor had merely smirked and led the way from Alex's tower to the throne room.

"I'm never using Dark alchemy," Alex had said firmly as he took up the allocated position on one side of the crossing. The Emperor had faced him, his robes rippling slightly in the gale rattling the stained glass windows.

"We shall see about that." And he had raised his arms. The hundreds of candles beside the throne had leapt up and combined into a single indigo-black pillar, sweeping across the chamber and striking like a gargantuan cobra. Alex's conjured diamond of protective light had shattered like brittle glass under the inferno's intensity.

He rolled onto his back, panting heavily. The dark

fire was still there, now more like a shark, circling overhead. Gasping with pain, he tried to reach for the alchemical power again.

"Do not try to heal yourself," the Emperor bellowed. "Don't get rid of the pain. Channel it . . . I said *no*."

Light had begun to shimmer around Alex's arm and course down the burn on his thigh. With a noise like a whip crack, the sharklike flame dived and speared his bicep. Alex howled again, and his attempt at alchemy faded.

"Now get up."

Groaning, he hoisted himself onto his good arm and tried to stand. It took a couple of tries, but he managed, staggering up to lopsidedly face his captor.

"Well, go on."

Alex glanced around, assessing what elements he had to work with. He caught sight of the window above the Emperor and raised his good arm, palm like a knife. The window shattered, and the wind entered properly. Alex focused and willed it downwards, compressing it, hammering it upon his adversary like a boulder.

"You think I am a fool? You think I can't see *Light*?"

A dome of crackling Dark energy had formed over the Emperor's head, and now it inverted, encasing the wind within a sphere.

The Emperor clicked, and the sphere was tossed over towards Alex. The impact was like being smashed with concrete, accompanied by an electric charge that set his nerve endings alight. He fell to his knees, retching.

"I won't use it," he said quietly after a long time breathing.

"We will continue this exercise until you do."

the black rose

"Well, you might as well kill me now, because I'm not going to."

"Really?" The Emperor had adopted his insidious rhetorical tone again. "You obviously know enough about Dark alchemy to understand it is formed from internal emotions rather than external elements. I'm sure we can coax it out of you."

Alex *did* know about Dark alchemy. He had seen the damage it had wreaked across the worlds he'd visited, including his own. To cave in and use it would make him just as bad as the Cult. "I refuse."

"That does not make you noble. It makes you weak. You have always been weak. Just as you couldn't stop your father beating your mother to death when you were seven, so you cannot defend yourself now."

Alex looked at him sharply. "You know nothing about that."

"On the contrary, I know everything about that. Or what about the casual drug abuse of your early teenage years?"

Alex was breathing heavily again but this time not out of physical pain. His stomach seemed to flip with the return of memories he had fought so hard to suppress.

"Or your friend Connor, so dear to you, who you were unable to protect from something as mundane as a speeding car?"

"Shut up." The rage swelled, scouring his insides, threatening to spew from his throat with searing venom.

"Or your undisclosed lifestyle choice, kept concealed with such care?"

74

"Shut up." He was dimly aware of the breeze beginning to pick up around him.

"Is *that* what you so very much wanted to tell Mister Lawson the night you returned to Earth—?"

"*Shut up!*"

He felt his control escape into the shadows of his mind. A tornado, laced with indigo darts, exploded outwards from around him in all directions, shattering all the remaining windows. The vaults of the crossing were filled with a tremendous rumbling as the fragments clattered to the marble floor.

Alex collapsed, utterly spent. Amongst the torrent of broken glass, the Emperor smirked. "Now we're getting somewhere."

Four days after their arrival at the goblin camp, the priest had returned. It was midmorning, and Lucy had been playing with Doch outside Maht's tent: a game of the girl's own invention, which seemed to be something like a cross between hide-and-seek and a doll's tea party but with the players inexplicably transforming into pterodactyl kittens at random intervals.

Adâ had jogged down the path, waving like a madwoman. Though she might not have done exactly the same, Lucy shared her feeling of urgency: she wasn't going to miss out on what they'd been waiting for. She deposited Doch with her mother inside and called a few disconnected words of explanation as she ran off towards the center of the camp.

Sipping from a wooden cup, the priest sat cross-legged to the right of the matriarch, his layers of furs rivaling hers. Like her, he was immensely old.

Lucy joined Adâ, Hakim, and Vince on the floor.

Hakim began to speak, but the priest waved him into silence with a frail hand. "The matriarch has explained your wishes to me. We shall go to the Cave. In fact, we shall leave right away."

Everyone looked round at him, alarmed, including the matriarch, who evidently saw fit to intervene. "Your Grace, surely your travel has tired you? You must wait a few days and rest—"

With the same rather irritating motion, the priest quieted her. "I am quite well." He stood, finished his drink, and turned to the Apollonians. "Collect your belongings and meet me at the northern gate." He nodded to the matriarch and departed.

There was silence as everyone recovered from the abrupt decree.

Then the matriarch spoke again. "It is, of course, the priest's decision to lead you to the Cave, and I cannot impinge on that. However, something is not right with him. You must keep an eye on him whilst you travel and ensure he comes to no harm."

The four of them nodded and stood to leave.

Chapter X
espionage

The smog-studded mist had descended once more as Jack, Sardâr, Bál, and Ruth crept through the lamp-lit streets of Albion. They had waited until past midnight, guaranteeing that the last servants would have departed and that the Osbornes would be immobilized by sleep and several superfluous layers of bedsheets.

For the first time in over a week, the four of them had washed thoroughly. Sardâr had rightly pointed out that if they hoped to remain undetected, trailing grime in and out of the house probably wasn't a good idea. However, the dirt's resilience had been unpleasantly surprising. By the time Jack had finished flaking off soot, the air of the factory and the entire city had seemed to crawl under his skin again. He looked forward to a proper shower aboard *The Golden Turtle*.

The corn-yellow moon swooped between chimneys as they approached the Osborne Manor. All the lights appeared to be off and all the curtains drawn.

Ruth led them down a driveway to the left and, withdrawing a thick ring of keys from her belt, unshackled the cast-iron gates. They slipped inside, careful not to let the metal clang, and made their way across the darkened courtyard to the interior door. Ruth repeated the action with a different key, and they were in the house.

Jack peered into the gloom as the door was closed behind him. They were in a servant's utility or laundry room, with folded piles of clothes loaded on shelves around them.

Ruth crept into the next room, and they followed in single file: through the kitchen with its monstrous stone that reminded Jack of the orphanage back on Earth, up spiral steps in the opposite corner of the dining room, past a colossal wooden table to the main hallway. The front door was directly opposite them at the end of a long Oriental rug. Flickering light shimmered through a curtained window, falling on the banisters of the main staircase.

They reached the top, and Ruth was about to set foot on the carpet, but Sardâr held her back. Silently, and without leaving the stairs, he crouched and examined the floor. He muttered a few syllables and passed his hand a few inches above the weaving. A projection of the floor, carpet threads cast in indigo light, rose from its real counterpart and vanished into the air.

"Alchemical alarm now disabled," Sardâr whispered, straightening and proceeding. They came to the first door on the left and the elf pressed his palm to it, light flashing and receding, to unlock it.

Ruth eased it open, and they entered.

Sardâr raised his arms, and the lamps flickered to life. The drawing room was exactly as Ruth had left it: icicles clinging to the plastered ceiling and hanging off the overstuffed furniture, frost clasping the wallpaper and curtains.

Even under his overcoat, Jack shivered. "Why is it so cold in here?" It was then that he saw what Ruth had described.

Behind the desk, where a portrait might have hung, a slab of ice the size of a fridge was set into the wall. Encased in it, apparently completely frozen, was a girl in what, inexplicably, appeared to be hiking wear.

"She's an elf," he whispered, noticing the pointed ears and Middle Eastern complexion. "Is she alive?"

"I think so," Sardâr replied, examining the frosty surface. "Otherwise there would be no point keeping her frozen. But we can deal with her in a minute. First, we should find what the Cult is up to."

Sardâr made his way to the desk and thumbed through the papers. Ruth joined him, indicating where she'd already looked and pointing out the locked drawers. Jack and Bál hung back, checking the door every few seconds with paranoid glances.

Sardâr beckoned them with a hiss. Jack and Bál almost stumbled over a footstool in their haste to get around the desk. The three others leaned in to see. The elf was holding up what seemed to be blueprints of a machine that reminded Jack of something from an H. G. Wells novel: a large sphere suspended above the ground by thin legs, extruding various spindly limbs—a kind of futuristic hunter spider. The only writing was a monogram printed in the corner.

"What does FGM stand for?"

"Frederick Goodwin Manufacturing," a voice answered from the doorway.

The four intruders looked up in shock.

Standing at the door, covered in a flowery nightgown and clasping a candelabra, was a middle-aged woman. Her hawkish eyes were fixed on them not with surprise but with something a little too close to hatred.

"Milady!" Ruth exclaimed. "Begging your pardon, but we were just, erm—"

"I don't think the formalities are necessary, Ruth," Sardâr said coldly, staring at the woman.

Jack felt it too. It was the same sensation he had when he saw a member of the Cult of Dionysus. There was something else there, a demonic presence his brain didn't want to recognize.

"Well observed, elf," the woman replied. In an instant her dress was gone, replaced by a hooded black cloak. Gone too was the candelabra. Instead, her hand was twisted as if she gripped a chalice, a cloud of ice-blue energy hovering in the center.

"Archbishop Nimue, I presume?"

"Correct, sir. And I believe you are the now somewhat legendary Sardâr Râhnamâ, leader of the Apollonians, who so aggravated the fortunes of the late Iago?"

"Indeed."

"I must say," Nimue continued, her aristocratic manners apparently unchanged by the removal of her disguise, "it is a genuine pleasure to share conversation with other Enlightened folk." She swaggered across the room to seat herself in one of the high armchairs, which had now transfigured into a throne of ice. "We had a maid who happened to overhear a little too much yesterday and, well, fate didn't smile upon *her*—"

"What's this?" Sardâr asked coolly, ignoring the elitist jibes and holding up the blueprints.

Nimue laughed: a high soporific tinkling. "Enlightened but nonetheless ignorant. Do you really think it was pure coincidence that you all ended up employed by us or our associates? Iago's losing possession of his mirror only lowered him in our estimation. If he had not already suffered the worst punishment imaginable, it would have been multiplied a hundredfold. However, we know what you have seen of us. We made sure you were channeled into places where we could watch you until our work here was done. And here you are, and you are too late."

"You still haven't answered my question," Sardâr replied, his voice rising.

Nimue laughed again. "This isn't a novel. I'm not some tragically flawed supervillain who'll tell you all my plans on the off chance you won't survive. Suffice it to say, though, you shall not be around to see them come to fruition."

She rose from her throne into the air like a banshee,

lifted on alchemical winds which were now redirected upon the Apollonians. Jack stumbled against the growing gale drawing him into the center of the room, the cord of the Seventh Shard cutting into his neck as it was pulled towards Nimue's hand. On the other side of the desk, Bál struggled against the same alchemical force, the First Shard drawing closer to the Cultist's other hand.

Sardâr leapt onto the table and bellowed another alchemical command. Instantly, the wind ceased and the room was filled with alabaster light as glowing weapons flashed into each of their grasps: swords for Jack and Sardâr, an axe for Bál, and a spear for Ruth.

Nimue's gaze narrowed. "This grows tiresome. I am running on a tight schedule. We shall have to extract the more valuable artifacts from the wreckage upon our return."

There was a deep rumbling, and Sardâr ducked as the slab of ice was rent from its socket on the wall, the frozen girl pulled through the air to float beside Nimue. Before any of them could react, the Cultist had flung a fireball to the floor, where it surged upwards. Indigo flames licked the walls and furnishings, forming a superheated wall between the two sides.

Nimue raised her hand, the familiar, thorny rose lacing over it, and vanished in a swirl of black smoke.

Jack summoned his energy and held his palms up, drawing upon the moisture in the air. A sphere of water formed between his hands and catapulted into the heart of the fire. He waited expectantly for a hiss of vapor, but none came. Instead, the flames rose even higher.

"It's *Dark* alchemy," Sardâr called over the crackling.

"We need something stronger."

Bál raised his newly conjured axe. "We'll try something else, then." He tensed his forearm, and a thick wreath of crimson flame unfurled from the end of the weapon, arching into the purple wall.

Jack's surprise at the dwarf's willingness to resort to alchemy was quickly outdone by his dismay at its complete lack of effect. The wave of indigo engulfed the crimson, growing even stronger.

"What are we going to do?" Ruth exclaimed.

With a loud crack, part of the floor collapsed, remnants of flaming furniture tumbling into the dark hole that had opened.

The four of them backed against the wall, and Sardâr began focusing bright light between his hands. Every few seconds, more of the floor disappeared in a flurry of sparks. The hideous furnishings had been nearly consumed; only increasingly charred plaster and wood remained.

Yells could be heard from the window near Jack. He leaned over and peered between the curtains at the street below. People were emerging from other houses on the street, staring up at the incendiary manor. As he watched, a wagon pulled up in front of the gates and a few navy-coated men clambered out to direct civilians away from the fire.

Sardâr's cry of pain pulled Jack's gaze back into the room. Loosened by the flames, a section of ceiling had collapsed, crushing one of the elf's legs. The light between his hands flickered and faded. The flames, seeming to sense this, took their chance. They began slithering over to him and wrapped their cords around his limbs, pulling him into the roaring fire.

Ruth and Bál took an arm each and hauled him back.

"This way," Jack shouted, ripping aside the curtains and yanking the window open.

"We can't jump from here," Ruth screamed, joining him at the window.

"What choice have we got?" Jack shouted.

The flames had consumed most of the room, leaving them with only a shrinking island behind the desk. Within moments, the desk was gone too, sliding into the corona oblivion below. Under other circumstances, Jack could have used the Seventh Shard to overcome this alchemy, but he knew that was exactly what Nimue wanted—for them to put out the fire and deal with the consequences whilst she continued with her plans unimpeded. At that moment, they had to flee rather than fight.

Jack and Ruth joined Bál in pulling Sardâr to his feet and assisting him to the window. Jack looked at the three sooty faces: Bál nodding, resolute; Ruth shaking her head, terrified; Sardâr grimacing, pained. He looked through the second-story window at the pavement below.

They jumped.

Perhaps naturally for someone who'd grown up on a steady diet of James Bond and *Die Hard*, Jack still retained some faith that leaping several meters down onto stone would be fine and would not hurt. It wasn't, and it did.

He hit the ground on his side and heard a couple of snaps, nuclear agony exploding across his upper body. He had spent three weeks in combat training, been hit by Dark alchemical lightning, and journeyed in and out of a volcano, and this still factored high on the pain scale. He tried to pull himself to his feet but was unable. He couldn't move his left arm at all, and even lifting his neck shot arrows across his nerves.

All he could see were the boots of those navy-coated men marching towards them. Ruth and Bál's explanations turned to cries of protest as they were hauled to the wagon. The dwarf's struggle was proving too much for the captor, but Bál was soon restrained by several more whilst one beat him to his knees with a truncheon.

Jack recognized his own voice shouting just as he felt a force on his shoulders. He was being dragged across the road towards the same wagon, his wounded arm scraping the street.

The pain was too much. He blacked out.

Chapter XI
the slammer

Jack became aware of the pain before he properly woke. As he rose out of the depths of his unconscious mind, the dull ache grew stronger and stronger, until he could feel he was lying on a hard surface. His eyes flicked open, and he got his first look at the room.

It was a small chamber constructed entirely of stone: underground, it seemed, by the way the barred window was crammed in the very top corner. The only light—that of the fog-masked moon and flickering street lamps—filtered through these bars, and from this Jack could just about make out the scene.

Sardâr lay on a bench opposite him, unconscious, whilst Bál slumped on the floor rubbing his truncheon wounds. Ruth, the only one who looked unharmed, was standing, apparently unable to keep still. Seeing he was awake, she flurried over to him.

"Don't even think about it," she said as he prepared to hoist himself up. She smiled and stroked his hair lightly.

Despite the situation, he was struck again by how beautiful she was: her skin the tone and texture of warm chocolate, her eyes like large onyx jewels set in milky oases. The pain seemed to have made everything a little more poetic. He felt the almost euphoric urge to slide his fingers around the base of her neck and press his lips to hers.

The face of an irate dwarf plugged the empty space in Jack's vision, somewhat ruining the moment. "Have you learnt any healing alchemy yet?" Bál said.

"No," Jack replied, trying to restrain his annoyance, "but I guess I can give it a go." Trying to stave off the pain a little longer, he placed his right hand on the dwarf's shoulder and closed his eyes. He knew healing alchemy was tied to Light, and so he focused on accumulating the powers of the different elements around him: the street lamps for fire, the dampness for water and air, the stone benches for earth. He channeled all of this into the Seventh Shard. Seeing it shining even through his eyelids, he allowed it to flow down his right arm into the dwarf.

He opened his eyes.

Bál felt his bruises again. They seemed to have faded considerably.

"Great, now try you," Ruth said.

Jack looked down at his limp left arm. He thought he'd probably pass out again if he tried to move it. It looked broken in two places, judging by the way he seemed to have mutated additional joints on the bicep and below the wrist. A month ago, he reflected, this would have been monumental. Now, though, it seemed an expectable part of the whole sorcerer-fighting experience.

He placed his good hand on the bad arm and closed his eyes again, summoning the same elements as before and channeling them through the Shard. It was much harder this time, not only because his energy was diminished but also because broken bones were a much bigger deal than bruising.

He opened his eyes. The breaks seemed to be gone his left arm was smooth—but something was wrong. He swung his legs down from the bench to sit up straight. There was only a slight twinge of pain, but he could feel the healed arm was now several inches shorter than the other one.

"How does it feel?" Ruth asked sympathetically, clearly having noticed the difference.

"It's okay. It'll have to do until Sardâr can take a proper look at it. Is he okay?"

"I hope so. He's breathing, but that dark fire stuff can't have done any good."

Jack got up and checked the elf's breathing. His face was pale and plastered with sweat, and he winced even in sleep.

"So this is prison, then? How long have we been here?"

"I don't think this is actual prison. I think it's just a jail cell. And I'm not sure how long we've been here. A few hours, maybe?" Ruth, sitting with her knees to her chest, looked anxious. Jack remembered she'd been imprisoned in Nexus: their current predicament couldn't be doing much to assuage her panic.

"So how do we get out, then?" Bál demanded.

Jack had to suppress another flare of annoyance. They were all in this cell. Just because Bál, a member of a royal family, had enjoyed free rein all his life didn't make this experience any worse for him than for anyone else.

"I don't know," Jack said. "We can't do much until Sardâr wakes up. I don't really want to try any alchemy on him. I'm not sure exactly what's wrong with him. Ruth, don't you have that egg for *The Golden Turtle*? Can't you call up the crew?"

Ruth shook her head sadly and produced a mangled mechanism from her pocket. "It shattered in the fall. Ishmael gave that to me too."

They passed the next few hours in uneasy silence. Jack put an arm around Ruth, and she rested her head on his lap. The cell stank—an unpleasant combination of urine and stale food that, contrary to expectations, seemed to become *more* noticeable the longer they stayed. Sardâr didn't move at all. Though very uncomfortable against the stone, Jack eventually followed the other two into sleep.

After some imperceptible amount of time, Ruth shook him awake. She was sitting bolt upright, pointing at the barred window.

Blinking to adjust to the darkness of the cell, he tried to see what she was gesturing at. Something obscured the streetlight: a crouching figure, rattling the bars.

Bál awoke with a start and, as if by instinct, reached for his axe.

Jack stood and, motioning the others to stay back, crept towards the window. "Hello?"

The figure drew out what looked like a glowing green wire from somewhere. There was a noise like a buzz saw, and the remnants of the bars jangled on the cell floor.

"Quickly," hissed a Cockney voice, "someone will've heard that." A rope was slung down to him.

Jack glanced into the cell, held up an index finger to Ruth and Bál, and proceeded to ascend the rope. It was a mark of his recent burst of fitness that he was able to do this with an injured arm: being bellowed at for his inability to climb a rope had been a recurrent feature of PE classes.

He pulled himself through the window, trying not to scrape the remaining edges of bars, and hauled himself to his feet. They were in a side alley, and the first vestiges of daylight were breaking over the soot-encrusted sky.

Jack looked at his rescuer and started. It was the boy from the factory. "Dannie! What are you doing here? I mean, it's great, but how—?"

"We'll have plenty of time to talk in a minute," the boy replied, "but let's just get your friends out first. Oh, and there's something you should probably know." Dannie pulled off his flat cap, and a tightly concealed bundle of dirty-blonde hair was let loose. "It's actually Danielle, but the name Dannie's fine."

the black rose

Jack stared at her blankly for a moment. "Erm, okay then. Let's help the others up."

Getting Ruth and Bál out was easy, particularly once the dwarf got over the initial surprise of being rescued by a factory colleague . . . who'd turned out to be a girl.

Sardâr was more difficult. Whatever was wrong with him, he wouldn't wake up, so they had to find a way to maneuver him out of a window that was practically on the ceiling. In the end, they managed it by Bál supporting the elf's weight whilst Jack levitated him out alchemically. It looked a little like an alien abduction.

"Right, so where are we going? Back to The Kestrel's Quill?"

Ruth shook her head. "No point. The Cult will have left the city by now. And there's the small problem of us now being bankrupt escaped convicts. I think we should head back to *The Golden Turtle*."

They made their way down to the river as quickly and quietly as they could, a job made much harder because they had to carry Sardâr like a corpse. To any passersby, Jack thought they must have looked very suspicious.

The rising sun shimmered through the clouds of smoke and reflected off the rain-smeared rooftops as the river came in sight. The early risers were already up, including a newspaper vendor. Ruth peered round the corner of an alley to see her own face—badly rendered and made to look older and nastier—glaring at her from the front of a newspaper.

It was next to similar portraits of Jack, Bál, and Sardâr under a thickly printed headline:

92

THIEVERY AND ARSON AT CITY MANOR

She waited until the vendor was distracted selling a paper, then signalled for the other three to follow her across the road. Jack and Bál hobbled along with a limp, Sardâr clutched between them.

"I guess we won't be coming back here anytime soon," Jack said as they reached the riverbank.

"What a tragedy," Bál replied darkly.

The Golden Turtle was exactly where they had left it— or, rather, the rail surrounding the top hatch was still floating unnoticed several feet from the bank. Ruth dived in, followed by Dannie and then Jack and Bál, who dragged Sardâr through the water as if they were towing a kayak.

Ruth scrambled onto the railing and pulled open the hatch. Dannie hopped in after her. Bál lowered Sardâr to them and climbed down. Jack took one last look at the filthy city rising from the riverbank and followed Bál, not at all regretting their departure from Albion.

Chapter XII
dannie

The first thing they attended to was Sardâr. Dripping river water all the way through the ship, Jack and Bál carried him to the command deck and laid him out on the map table.

Ruth had summoned Quentin, who apparently, in addition to being first mate, was the ship's doctor. He had brought a large leather case, which he set next to the elf's legs and opened to reveal a plethora of implements. Affixing a pair of thick-lensed spectacles to his nose, he made a set of initial observations before speaking.

"The fellow's been hit by some kind of Dark alchemy," Quentin confirmed in his natural Etonian accent, for once making no attempt to sound pirate-like. "I need to give him a rather strong stimulant to wake him." He searched his case and retrieved a syringe. Emptying a vial of clear liquid into it, he tested it and raised it over the elf's body.

"He's not going to enjoy this," Quentin remarked drily and punctured Sardâr's breastbone.

The elf snapped up into a ninety-degree position, inhaling sharply, his eyes open so wide that white could be seen all around his pupils. It took several minutes for his breathing to return to normal, at which point he thanked Quentin with a pat on the shoulder.

"You can't keep on like this, old chap," Quentin reprimanded him. "All these damn scrapes you get yourself into. First the incident in the volcano, then that nasty business with Zâlem, now this. Your body can only take so much alchemical injury before it snaps for good."

Satisfied that Sardâr was going to remain conscious, they all took a break to get cleaned up and changed. Jack was given a renewed sense of just how much soot and oil had become encased in his skin. After a long shower and having changed his filthy shirt and trousers for the tunic he'd worn as an elf, he felt a lot more comfortable.

Whilst running a towel through his hair, which had grown much longer in the weeks since he'd left Earth, he took stock of his belongings. The Albion clothes were in a pile ready to be taken to the laundry room and perhaps added to Quentin's theatrical collection from different worlds. His bag still held a selection of toiletries snatched from his room in Thorin Salr, which he had emptied onto his bed. The really important stuff was now on his person. The gauntlet from the goblin Vodnik, awarded to Jack for saving his life, was clasped onto his left fore-arm. The language ring was on the fourth finger of his left hand. The Seventh Shard, as always, was threaded around his neck under his tunic.

He glanced at the bed absently, half-expecting to see Inari there, but, of course, he had sent the fox to keep an eye on Lucy. The pang of guilt surprised him: she had barely been in his thoughts. It *had* been less than a fortnight since they'd parted ways, and though she'd been away on family holidays longer than this, it seemed like a lifetime since he'd seen her.

He joined the group on the command deck. The water they'd spread into the room had been mopped up, and everything looked just as they'd left it a little over a week ago: banks of high-tech computer monitors, murky water beyond the glass, and the large oak table in the center, where Ruth, Sardâr, Bál, and Dannie stood.

"About time," Ruth said as he approached. "We were wondering what had happened to you."

They were all looking down at a piece of paper. "I managed to take this from the desk in Osborne Manor," Sardâr explained. "We think it shows where they might be going. Can you read this, please?"

Jack leaned to have a look, wondering why it had to be him. The map was very minimalist, with a few lines showing the city and a river running eastwards. A route had been traced westwards from the city to a forest upriver. An X was marked in a glade of trees, and a single word had been scrawled in thin handwriting. "It says *commune*."

"What does that mean?" Dannie asked.

"I'm not exactly sure," Sardâr replied, for some reason still appraising Jack. "Though we know from our look into the black mirror that Nimue was searching for the fairies of this world who supposedly guard the Third Shard. We have yet to discover why she ended up in a human city instead. We know from those plans that they've constructed some kind of machine. I think if we follow them to this commune, we'll find out more."

All of them nodded.

Sardâr handed the map to one of the crew members operating the computer consoles. Moments later, bubbles were rising beyond the glass dome as the ship dived and began its journey upriver.

"Now," Ruth said, rounding on Dannie, "*you've* got some questions to answer."

Dannie smiled sheepishly. "Fair enough. I haven't really explained anything."

"So you work in the Goodwin factory?" Jack prompted, trying to temper Ruth's accusatory tone. "But why did you rescue us? And, for that matter, how did you know where to find us?"

Dannie grinned now, and the phrase *grease monkey* found its way into Jack's head. She was fairly short and very thin, skin still thick with ingrained dirt even after a shower, and her shoulder-length blonde hair fell in oily curls around her tanned face. She had opted to keep her own clothes, and, despite the new revelations about her gender, the boots, trousers, shirt, and flat cap suited her.

"Well, I *am* a factory worker, but I guess I'm a sort of detective as well. It's a long old story, but I'll give you the short version. My dad was a laborer for this small manufacturing firm. It was a pretty good setup, but then Fred

Goodwin bought it out and fired the whole workforce. That pretty much did Dad in. So when I was old enough, I decided to get back at Goodwin. I've been investigating his operation for a while now, trying to dig up some of the dirt everyone knows is there but no one can find any hard evidence for. So I was working undercover at the factory.

"Then, just over a week ago now, this Osborne woman shows up and a lot of manufacturing firms' profits practically double overnight, including Goodwin's. Very shady. So I do a bit more digging and find that someone else is asking the same questions as me"—she nodded at Sardâr—"and so I kept an eye on you. I followed you to the Osborne place and saw you jump out of that flaming window. And then the bobbies got you. Of course, I didn't know you were all connected until then!" She pointed between Sardâr, Jack, and Bál.

"But what took you so long to get to the prison? We were there for hours!"

"I lost track of the paddy wagon, so I had to go round all the police stations in the city searching for you. You were in the fourth or fifth one I tried. Nearly got it badly wrong a few times. I'd got the rope down on one before I realized I was busting out a deranged murderer! Now *that* would've been a mistake . . ."

"And so you're coming with us now?"

"May as well. I'm interested to see what this Osborne woman's up to. If I can catch her, I've got a good chance of pinning something on Goodwin."

Jack had half-expected this. Dannie was well-intentioned and sharp, but she clearly had no idea who was really behind all this. He nodded his assent to Sardâr, and he saw Ruth and Bál do the same.

The elf smiled exasperatedly. "Well, it would be me doing the explaining, wouldn't it? Very well. Dannie, there are some things you should know before we get to the forest . . ."

Sardâr told her everything—or at least everything Jack knew: about the different races and worlds; about the Apollonians and the Cult; about the Cult's plan to create a superweapon; about the legends Isaac had come across; about the Shards of the Risa Star and an Übermensch and the race to find them.

For the most part, Dannie took it surprisingly well. Considering that for Jack and Lucy to be convinced, it had taken a Cult attack on their home, being transported to another world, and fighting a demon inside a volcano. Dannie, conversely, was positively nonchalant about the whole thing.

"So," she said, once Sardâr had finished and she'd computed everything for a few seconds, "you're an elf, you're a dwarf, you're a human—so what are you?" She looked lastly at Ruth, who looked back at her, confused.

It was then that Jack caught sight of a new golden egg set upon one of the maps—a replacement for the one that had shattered outside the manor. It made him remember something. "Dannie, what was it you used to get us out of the cell?"

Dannie grinned again and rolled up her shirt slightly, undoing a thick leather belt from around her waist and laying it out on the table. It held a line of various metal implements, like a mechanic's tool kit. She unclipped what looked like a pair of skipping rope handles.

"Pulse wire," she explained, pulling the handles apart to reveal a thin line of green energy between them. "Can cut through pretty much anything, including prison bars."

"What else have you got in there?" Ruth asked, obviously impressed.

Dannie replaced the pulse wire and pulled out something that looked like a cross between a key and a screwdriver. "Thunder key. Sends an electric pulse through a lock to align the tumblers. And my personal favorite." She swapped the key for a small pistol. "Memory gun. A blast from this and you'll be hazy for about five minutes . . . until you realize your incriminating documents have been swiped from your safe."

"And where did you get all this?" Sardâr inquired coolly. It was the same reproachful tone he had adopted toward King Thorin when he'd suspected that explosives had been stolen from another world.

"I made them. Alchemically enhanced technology. Like this whole place, right?" She gestured around at the innards of the ship.

Ruth raised her eyebrows. "I think you're going to fit in around here."

Chapter XIII
the cave of lights

The journey to the Cave of Lights was the toughest challenge Lucy had ever faced. Leaving the goblin encampment, they had struck out north across the frozen plains, crossing the river via an ancient-looking bridge—provoking a twinge of memory of Thorin Salr—and begun the long ascent.

Snow fell in the foothills and continued once they reached the mountains proper. Each night they went to sleep amidst a scene of silently descending flakes, and in the mornings they awoke to a fresh layer of white all around them. The tribe had lent them a couple of smaller tents, one for Lucy and Adâ and another for Hakim and Vince. These were notoriously difficult to set up and disassemble, so they allowed an additional hour at sunrise and sunset to do so. The days were freezing, and the nights were even colder. They ate what little they had brought—mainly dry food from Maht's store—in two small meals each day around an alchemically conjured fire.

They barely spoke for the entire journey, all of them silently acknowledging that words would waste energy they sorely needed. The air became noticeably thinner the higher they climbed, and it took considerable effort for all of them to continue moving at a steady pace. Their priest guide had said not a single word since leaving the matriarch's tent but shuffled always several feet ahead of them, forging a shallow causeway through the snow.

Lucy, like her three companions, had piled on as many layers as possible before departure. She was aching now from the daylong periods of hiking, and she had almost lost all feeling in her extremities. When she removed her gloves, it was to find her fingertips had turned black. One evening, as they were eating, she had shown Hakim. The elf had grimaced and, placing his fingertips to hers, proceeded to heal her with alchemy. This was fine until she noticed later that, rather than disappearing, the frostbite seemed to have transferred to him. She felt instantly guilty and resolved to keep it to herself in the future.

To her slight surprise, her thoughts were not mostly occupied by Jack or even Alex but by Maht. They had shared the briefest of good-byes before she had left, when the goblin had pulled her into a swift hug and wished her good luck. Lucy felt nothing but admiration for the single mother raising her daughter alone. As soon as she was able to, she intended to honor her last

104

words to Maht: "I'll come back for you."

Night was approaching on the fourth day when they finally crossed a ridge and reached the temple. The sun rippled bloodred through the watery sky, approaching the western horizon and elongating their fur-plumped figures into skeletal shadows. The entrance to the Cave of Lights was three human-sized slabs of stone, marking a gloomy opening in the mountainside. There was nothing to distinguish it from anything else in the arctic range. Lucy couldn't see what was particularly *lit* about it.

"So this is it, then." Vince panted, knocking patronizingly on the doorway. "Not an easy place to find, is it?"

"I think that's the point," Adâ replied, joining him. The elf looked particularly ridiculous in all those furs, something like a giant cotton ball.

Hakim exchanged a few words with the goblin priest and then pulled the three Apollonians into a huddle slightly away from the entrance. "We need to be on our guard going in there," he said quietly. "By now, the Cult will have had time to get in and possibly even take the Shard. We don't know what might be waiting for us."

"Yeah," Lucy added, unable to resist, "what does this remind you of?"

Hakim and Adâ winced, clearly remembering Mount Fafnir.

"Very well," Hakim addressed the priest as they returned to the entrance, "could you lead us inside?"

The tunnel they entered was completely black. Hakim conjured a fireball to hover in his palm, sending flickering orange light to illuminate the rough-hewn walls. They moved downwards with no indication of when the passage would end until, finally, a glimmer became visible in front of them. They continued in single file until they reached another high doorway, and it opened out.

Lucy wasn't sure what she was seeing. She initially thought they were outside again, but that wasn't possible; they had been moving downwards all the time. It took her several seconds to realize what she saw was not a starlit sky but a colossal underground chamber stretching the length of several football pitches. What she had taken for stars were actually floating lights, set in alcoves around the entire circular wall and up countless levels. The floor of the Cave seemed to be a massive lake, forming an exact mirror reflection of the lights above except for seven stone walkways from the wall to a small island in the center. She had visited cathedrals with her parents and never really understood them, but this was something else. For the first time, she began to understand why some people were religious.

"What are the lights?" she whispered to Hakim as they proceeded.

"I'm not exactly sure. This is only a guess, but I think there's one for every deceased goblin. I think it symbolizes them being led safely to the afterlife."

The priest had stopped on the edge of the island. Hakim passed him, followed by Lucy. The only thing on the island was a simple stone plinth, carved with star symbols. The other two joined them, and they huddled

The Cave of Lights

around to inspect it. The top was completely bare, save for a small hole in the center—a hole that would have exactly fitted a Shard of the Risa Star.

"Like rats to rancid butter," an unfamiliar voice echoed behind them.

They spun around.

A black-cloaked figure was standing on the walkway they had just come down, blocking their way back. But their attention was instantly distracted as the priest's form contorted and ripped out of the furs, leaving a snarling winged demon in its place.

"One point to me," crowed a female voice behind them.

The first figure tossed a coin over the island to a black-cloaked woman on the other side, and she caught it. "Paethon thought a doppelgänger could never fool you *again*, but I disagreed."

They both cackled.

"Phaedra and Paethon, I take it?" Vince asked coldly.

"Correct," they answered, and their voices slid together as one.

"Now," Paethon continued, "perhaps you can assist us. Where is the Shard?"

The Apollonians exchanged uncomprehending looks.

"We don't have the Shard," Hakim replied. "Don't you?"

Phaedra gave a theatrical sigh of contempt. "Now, is playing this game really worth our time? The plinth was empty when we arrived. We all know one of your meddlesome crew has it. If you're not going to give it up, then I'm afraid force is the only option."

Lucy could tell Adâ, Hakim, and Vince were also silently considering their options. There were only two Cultists, both surely powerful alchemists, but then so were Adâ and Hakim. They could probably take them and the demon down and run for the exit . . .

This plan was crushed by the materialization of five more Cultists in streams of black smoke, blocking all of the walkways.

"Keep close," Hakim muttered.

They had formed an outward-facing ring around the plinth, each of them eyeing the Cultists nearest them. Lucy, Adâ, and Vince instinctively moved their hands to the hilts of their swords, and Hakim reached for his wooden staff. Lucy was now considering the lake. They might be able to make a break for it and swim to the other side. If they distracted Paethon and jumped, they might just make it . . .

Lucy leapt back, alarmed, as waves began to roll over the surface of the water. They were gathering momentum, rising higher and higher when suddenly, with the roar of a waterfall, they blasted upwards. The black cloaks dissolved into smoke form as the water towered over the island, spinning like an aquatic tornado. The lights were now only blurred glimmers beyond the swiftly rotating wall.

The Apollonians were completely disoriented, all four of them looking frantically upwards, trying to catch a glimpse of ebony smoke. A bolt of dark lightning was hurled from somewhere above them, striking Hakim between the shoulder blades and knocking him flat.

Adâ flung an emerald jet in return, but it was lost in the swirling wall.

"Cowards!" Vince bellowed over the roaring water. He was hit by a blast in the shoulder, then another two in the stomach, and he crumpled to the ground.

Lucy and Adâ took up positions back to back. The elf conjured a humming golden ball, which she sent through the cyclone, momentarily illuminating the streaks of smoke. Both of them fired bolts, but the smoke streams were too quick and the water washed the golden orb away. A spike of Dark alchemy launched outwards from where it had faded, passing through Adâ's chest. She gasped, her eyes bulging, and collapsed on top of Vince.

Lucy leapt onto the pedestal. She knew she was more exposed here, but it afforded her a better chance of sighting the black cloaks' smoke. Through the rippling water, she saw one of the lights. Remembering what Jack had done back in Thorin Salr, she focused on it, channeling the light through her body. With the sound of an organ note, her dull metal sword burst into life, the blade shining incandescent white.

She was just in time. A wreath of dark flames blasted out to her left. She parried it with the alchemically infused weapon, flinging it back into the water. A scream of pain on the other side was accompanied by the thud of a body colliding with stone.

The tremendous roar of the whirlpool around her continued, but over it she could hear the screeching voice of Phaedra.

"My, she is a tenacious little sprite, isn't she?"

"I'm not sure." Paethon's voice resounded. "I doubt she'll be standing after a good old-fashioned drowning."

Phaedra cackled. "You're on!"

The very peak of the water wall rippled, turning inwards. The entire whirlpool was collapsing on the island.

Lucy's cry was immediately stifled by the torrent. She was knocked onto her back, the edge of the pedestal cutting a ridge in her spine as water hammered her. She gasped for breath but inhaled only foul liquid. She could see nothing; she could hear only the pounding of millions of droplets on stone. Her senses washed away, she passed out of consciousness like a sacrificial lamb on the altar as the black cloaks closed in.

The Cave of Lights

Chapter XIV
comforting words

True to Ruth's prediction, Dannie had settled right in. She was intrigued by the ship and spent hour upon hour exploring its every corridor and chamber. She often sat with the crew on the command deck discussing mechanics. But she didn't stop there. Less than three hours in, she was scrambling through chutes in the walls and under the carpet to examine the inner workings of *The Golden Turtle*. Dannie had an adaptability and buoyant optimism that Jack instinctively warmed to.

Sardâr, recovering from his latest alchemical injury, took things easier for those two days, mostly remaining in his room. As usual, Bál kept to himself. But Jack and Ruth passed the time with Dannie, soon finding they had something in common.

"So you're an orphan as well, then?" she asked Jack

after the three of them had been talking for a while.

"Join the club," Ruth remarked drily.

"How were things for you?" Dannie asked them both.

After Ruth explained about her amnesia, Jack began talking about his orphanage: that it had been in a depressing ex-prison and was chronically underfunded, though the staff had tried their best, and that he'd never really got on with the other children.

Dannie listened with raised eyebrows. "You think that's bad? You've never seen a workhouse." And by the time she'd related the squalor, the lingering hunger, the constant threat of disease, the staff's physical and mental abuse, the regular fights and occasional murder, Jack and Ruth's mouths were hanging open.

"Yep, you've definitely had the worst luck of us all," Ruth said weakly.

"Well, I don't know *for sure* whether I'm an orphan," Dannie qualified. "I never knew my mum; she disappeared pretty much as soon as I was out of her body. She might still be around somewhere, but I'm not fussed. As far as I'm concerned, I only had one parent."

Jack realized it was a mark of how much he liked Dannie that he wasn't annoyed that he couldn't be alone with Ruth. They hadn't spent any time together, just the two of them, since the previous Sunday, and the chances were increasingly unlikely with Ruth's renewed duties

Comforting Words

as captain of *The Golden Turtle*.

The first night, he had been so exhausted from factory work and their anti-Cult escapades that he'd been asleep as soon as he'd hit the bunk and for fourteen hours solid afterward. But the second, he found himself rolling over and over, each position less comfortable than the last, unable to rest his mind. His thoughts were on Lucy and Alex.

It had been over a week now since he had heard from Inari. He wondered if it was possible to summon the fox—he'd never tried it; the spirit had always appeared to him—but, he supposed, if there was nothing to report, then everything must be fine. He knew Lucy could look after herself, probably better than he could, but that didn't stop him from worrying about her or the three others with her, even though he didn't know them nearly as well. He imagined it must be something like how a big brother would feel towards a little sister.

In fact, he was much more concerned about Alex, who he'd received no news about at all since their departure from Earth six weeks ago. Jack agreed with Sardâr that Alex was probably still alive: Icarus wouldn't have gone to the trouble of abducting him unless he was more useful to the Cult alive than dead. But that introduced a whole new range of unpleasant ideas, like what the Cultists might do to get him to talk. He knew Alex was resilient, more so than anyone else he'd ever met, but how long could he hold out against Dark alchemy and demons? And if he had already cracked, would they just kill him as he was of no more use to them?

Finally, he gave up trying to sleep and went to see if Sardâr, in the next cabin, was awake. He knocked, and the elf called for him to come in.

As he entered, Jack was struck by a strong sense of déjà vu from the very first time the two of them had spoken at length, after Sardâr had been rescued from the heart of Mount Fafnir. The amber lights were low, shadows stretching across the floor and collecting in the corners of the cabin. The elf lay in bed, looking just as physically drained as he had after coming out of the volcano, his ochre eyes half-closed and his face drawn between curtains of grey-flecked dark hair. As before, Jack saw a strong semblance of a Zoroastrian priest in deep thought.

The elf beckoned him to sit on the end of the bed. "You couldn't sleep either, I take it?"

"Nope," Jack replied, leaning back against the wall.

"What's on your mind?"

Jack explained his concerns about Lucy and Alex.

"Yes, I miss Adâ too. And Hakim, obviously. And Vincent. But we haven't chosen an easy life, have we? I suppose it's up to us to sacrifice comfort and the close-ness of loved ones for the good of everyone else."

"I'm not complaining." Jack replied quickly. "I made my choice, the same as you. I had Lucy and Alex, but other than that I never really had any friends at home. But I've got friends in the Apollonians I wouldn't give up for anything. I've known you lot for such a short time, but still . . ." He was afraid he was becoming too senti-mental, but Sardâr smiled encouragingly.

114

"I'm glad you feel that way. Think of it like this: every Cult plot foiled, every Shard discovered is one step closer to reuniting with Lucy and freeing Alex. And maybe we Apollonians can spend some time together as friends rather than agents when this is all over."

Jack hadn't thought ahead to it being over. He was slightly surprised at the suggestion. So far, it had been about getting over the next hurdle, fighting the next demon, finding the next Shard. "I'd like that. I've never been on a proper holiday."

They were both silent for a moment before Jack built up the courage to ask the question burning on his lips. "So you think there can be an *all over*, then? You think we can beat the Cult for good, and that'll be that?"

Sardâr inhaled slowly, gazing at the ceiling. "Even if we stop the Cult, it won't be all finished. The Cult of Dionysus think they manipulate the Darkness, but the Darkness really manipulates them. That's their biggest folly. It's sheer arrogance for a group of mortals to think they can control a cosmic force which, as far as we know, has been around indefinitely. You already know that. We can bring an end to the Cult, but the Darkness will still seek to consume the Light, even if it doesn't have mortal pawns to act for it. That's why finding the Shards of the Risa Star is so important—not just to keep them from the Cult but because we rely on this Übermensch legend to bring an end to the Light-Dark conflict for good.

"If only we still had Isaac here . . ."

Sardâr's eyes clouded over, and Jack instantly regretted bringing up the elf's old friend. He didn't know what to say. "Were you close?"

"Yes, we were. Isaac, Charles, and I were the first Apollonians: three mortals from three different worlds. We were all, if you don't mind me saying, great minds, but Isaac was greatest of all. He invented the first of our dimension ships almost single-handedly—he and his brother Ishmael built *The Golden Turtle* together. And he had this way of inspiring people, of helping them believe that even when the future looks like an abyss, we *can* change the world for the better."

"He sounds very like you."

"You are very kind, but—"

"No, I mean it. I've seen it. People look to you for leadership; they're comforted by you being there. Do you think the Apollonians would have gone inside Mount Fafnir or into the middle of a battlefield just for any old person?"

Sardâr smiled again. "Thank you." He paused. "Jack, there's something you should probably know before we go any further. A suspicion of mine. It's only that at the moment, but even so—" He broke off. "No, don't worry. It can wait. We should probably both get some sleep."

Anxiety not entirely assuaged, Jack bid Sardâr good night and returned to his own room.

Their voyage ended two days after it had begun, when *The Golden Turtle* was at the closest part of the river to the destination marked on the map. The group departing the ship—Jack, Ruth, Dannie, Sardâr, and Bál—had, for lack of any other appropriate clothing, been equipped with Thorin Salr–style tunics, boots and cloaks, and, to the dwarf's relief, their swords. This time, without the need for stealth in a city center, they were able to lower the ramp so the five could scramble ashore without first soaking themselves in water.

"We can't have got here before the Cult, can we?" Ruth said to Sardâr, looking around the riverbank.

Jack silently seconded her caution. There was nothing to suggest anyone else had been here, but as they had found out before in a bad way, sight definitely wasn't a reliable sense when Dark alchemy was involved.

"We might well have," the elf replied, gazing at the trees. "Nimue may not have been able to travel using Darkness. The Cult back in Thorin Salr transported a bridge that way, but that was a fairly simple structure. Whatever this new machine they've built is, it looked a lot more complex . . ."

The forest stretched out before them, peaks of whispering green clustering up the rise from the river and rolling over hills in the distance. The sky was much clearer here than back in the city. Trails of frosted white laced across the azure sky, free from the excrement of smog-choked chimneys. In stark contrast to the stone and pummelled mud of the Albion streets, the ground beneath them here was springy and alive with grass and bracken. Gone, too, was the stench of charring that had stuck in their noses and throats for the entire time in the city. Here, they could breathe clearly again.

They moved up the rise and into the thick of the forest, following Sardâr's map reading. Jack was taken aback by the new surroundings. He had seen an orchard on Earth, but it had been circumvented on all sides by buildings, anything mildly threatening removed by generations of human locals. This place, he could tell, hadn't been manufactured at all. Pockets of uneven grass and leaves sprang up here and there around his feet, and clumps of moss clung to the sides of trees. Wild banks of stinging nettles and other flora considered unfashionable in civilized society were in the full throes of life all around. Fallen branches had been left as they were, becoming colonized by mushrooms and absorbed into the ground. It was enough to make any landscape gardener suffer a breakdown.

It might have been his imagination, but everything seemed greener here too. The sunlight filtering through the clustering canopy of leaves was dyed a brilliant patchwork of emerald and gold, speckled patterns darting with the breeze over the ground. It must have been late November or early December on Earth now, but here the world seemed in the thick of spring.

Sardâr led them up the rise and then down into a wide tree-covered valley. Several other landmarks had been indicated on the map, and they ticked them off as they passed: a narrow ravine, at the bottom of which a brook gurgled; a large tree stump in the shape of devil's horns; a ring of fungi-encrusted standing stones. Finally, after at least an hour's walk, they passed between two grassy banks and moved out of the cover of the trees.

They stood on the edge of a wide glade, trees surrounding them completely. The sun was directly above, set like a jewel in sapphire surroundings. It must have been about midday.

"It should be here," Sardâr said slowly, examining the map as he strode into the center of the ring. "The X is marked right here . . ."

The others began looking around. Other than that it was the first one they'd come across, the glade seemed entirely unremarkable. If possible, Jack thought, this area seemed the greenest and liveliest place yet: even in the shade of the trees, there was not an inch of bare earth where some life had not sprouted.

"Well, then what are we miss—?" Bál broke off his sentence with a gasp.

Jack wasn't listening. He had caught sight of something glimmering in the shadow of a sycamore. When he moved closer, it looked as though two toffee-colored jewels had been set into the bark, glinting in the sunlight. He blinked.

The pair of jewels blinked back.

Chapter XV
the sword in the stone

Jack stumbled, landing hard on his back. He stood and backpedalled as fast as he could. The others had retreated too. His eyes still fixed upon the tree, he grasped one of Ruth's arms for support. Even through the rush of panic, he still registered the brush of her warm fingers as they clasped his wrist for reassurance.

It wasn't only the sycamore. Even as they watched, more and more glints became visible out of the shadow of the canopies. The trunks themselves seemed to be liquefying, the entire structure maintaining its shape but the grain now flowing like ripples on water. Knots widened everywhere, and the very bark seemed to extrude itself from within, reaching outwards into the center of the glade. A twisted arm to the right, a gnarled leg to the left, branches rustling with the movement, and seconds later they were surrounded by a group of figures.

Even with a growing compendium of elves, dwarves, goblins, giants, and demons, Jack's brain seemed to be taking an extra long time to work out what he was seeing here. The figures before them were like trees but also like humanoids: their skin was bark, complete with moss and leafy branches, but there were definitely two arms and two legs on each of them. And, of course, the jewel eyes set into stumpy heads, all fixed upon them. It was as if the trees of the glade had been copied and pasted onto a human template.

Sardâr got to his feet slowly, eyes flicking between the tree figures. "It's alright; you can get up," he whispered. "They're not going to harm us—I think."

Jack did as he was told. The other three did the same. Even when Jack stood, the figures were tall. Of course—they were tree-sized.

"Which of you is in charge?" Sardâr ventured, glancing around the circle.

With much rustling, the figures looked among themselves in what seemed to be confusion. There was a crackling as a bark mouth opened, and words came like a breeze through autumnal branches—yet sounding to Jack distinctly Welsh.

"There's no one in charge. We're all equal here."

"Granted, but even

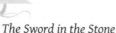

The Sword in the Stone

an egalitarian society predicates the appointment of an executive—"

Jack placed a silencing hand on Sardâr's shoulder. "You're fairies, aren't you?"

Several of the wood figures nodded slowly.

"How did you know that?" Ruth hissed, her eyes still on the surrounding figures.

"The black mirror. The Emperor mentioned fairies were here . . ." Jack had slightly surprised himself with his own memory. He had to admit, this wasn't what he'd been expecting. The fairies he'd known from childhood stories had been mouse-sized, with the build of ballerinas and glowing butterfly wings. What he now faced was as different from Tinker Bell as was possible.

"What brings you here?" a beech asked. "Few venture into our lands, and fewer still do so intentionally."

"We have come to speak with you of grave matters," Sardâr replied, "and to ask for your help."

"Then, please, sit with us and we'll speak," said a spruce.

Moments later, they were all seated in a circle in the glade. Whilst Jack was encouraged by their welcoming attitude, he was still disconcerted by the fairies' ability to blend into their surroundings. Each of them was now almost divided in two: the upper bodies had remained as trees but, below, the bark had subsided in favor of green blades, looking like emerald-furred goat legs.

Sardâr was kneeling, his cloak falling about his shoulder almost like folded wings as he addressed the circle. "Firstly, I must thank you for welcoming us into your abode. I wish that, in response to such hospitality, I bore good news, but I do not. Your realm is threatened by a great evil, which is approaching as we speak. A group of sorcerers who call themselves the Cult of Dionysus are set upon ravaging your lands and taking your most precious heirloom: the Third Shard of the Risa Star."

There was muttering around the circle.

"We've known for many years this day would come," a hawthorn replied, "but the Shard is not held dear by our people. It has wreaked its own havoc amongst us."

"Our ancestors were charged with its custodianship two thousand years ago," an oak continued, "and from the day it was entrusted to us, it has caused conflict. Our community has been repeatedly torn apart by struggles for control of its power."

"So where is it now?" Ruth interjected.

Many of the fairies exchanged looks.

"It is sealed. Hidden within this wood. Over half a millennium ago, our greatest alchemist, Merlin, sealed it within the forest so that only its rightful bearer, the one our ancestors were told would come for it, arrives."

"And that is the help we have come to ask for," Sardâr replied. "We are members of an organization called the Apollonians. We are searching for the Shards of the Risa Star and their rightful bearers in order to combat the threat posed by the Cult. We have come to ask for the Shard, and we can use it to help you defend your home."

"We will not fight this force that threatens us," one of the older elms said. "Everyone in this community has taken a vow of peace."

Jack exchanged surprised looks with Bál, Ruth, and Dannie. They hadn't exactly been expecting a group of tree-morphing pacifists.

"That is laudable," Sardâr continued, grimacing slightly, "but this is not some petty mortal conflict for pride or profit. We all face a Darkness which, if we do not unite, will engulf all our worlds. I implore you: you must defend yourselves and others by fighting off this evil."

"There is no evil which justifies taking up arms against another creature," a blackthorn intoned, as if reading from a textbook.

Several others around the circle nodded.

Sardâr had stood now, and his voice trembled. "This is not only about you! You could sacrifice your lives for a puritanical ideology if only *you* mattered, but there is far more at stake than this forest. You think if you lie down, the Cult will just roll over you and leave you alone. *They will not.* They will not stop until every tree in this entire world is burned down, and then they will move onto another world and another and another, strengthened by the Shard which you so graciously relinquished to them." He was shouting now, and a few birds fled from branches.

The majority of the fairies looked stunned; others just shook their heads. There was a renewal of murmuring.

"We must discuss this amongst ourselves," one of the fairies said. "Please, Apollonians, leave us whilst we decide."

The four other travelers joined Sardâr at the very edge of the glade. They sank down onto either side of the grassy bank. The elf was breathing heavily, his face reddened. Ruth looked a little alarmed. Bál rolled his head back and closed his eyes. Dannie busied herself going through her utility belt and cleaning inventions with a filthy cloth. The faint wind of fairy voices from the center of the glade could just be heard, though no words were discernible.

"Well, you were right about them not harming us . . ." Jack ventured after a few moments.

Sardâr rubbed his temple. "We had the same problem in Tâbesh. Our republic has had a bloody history too, and so there was a natural aversion to war, which was good. But when a threat arrives that *needs* to be stopped, what do you do? When Zâlem began to stir up racial trouble, a lot of people refused to make any move to counter him in case it turned violent. What they didn't see was that by doing nothing, they were just giving him free rein. And look what happened—he tried to assassinate the president. Isn't there any middle ground? These are almost the polar opposite of the fairies back on my world, who are fickle, spiteful, *always* ready to start a conflict—"

"And this is the elf who keeps having a go at people for racial stereotyping," Jack said coldly. He knew Sardâr was angry, but he didn't appreciate hypocrisy from someone he so looked up to.

The five of them sat in silence for a very long time. Then, after what must have been almost an hour, the circle of fairies beckoned them.

The elm addressed them. "We have reached an agreement. We will not fight these enemies who approach us.

126

We still believe that if we do not harm them, they will not harm us. However, we will guide you to the Shard's resting place. We have no love for that artifact. But we must warn you, only a rightful bearer will be able to draw it out of its prison and wield it."

Sardâr's eyes narrowed, but Jack spoke before Sardâr could. "Thank you. That's very helpful. Could you lead us there now, please?"

The fairies nodded.

The sycamore that had originally surprised Jack held out her branchy arm, and out of it a sphere of soft, pulsating light rose into life. "Follow this sprite. It will guide you to the Shard."

Jack nodded to the fairies and followed the sprite to the edge of the glade, where it bobbed, waiting.

Ruth, Bál, and Dannie did the same. Without looking back at the tree people, Sardâr came as well. The travelers moved toward the cover of trees, leaving the fairy commune behind.

They descended a steep slope, the canopy enclosing them once more. The sprite bobbed ahead, its ethereal glow highlighting bark and leaf in lemony light as they ventured through the vernal tunnel into the very heart of the forest.

Jack stumbled several times, sending showers of dirt and twigs into Ruth's back. He took to padding along as carefully as possible, trying not to slip.

Their surroundings became wilder as they moved down the hill, the pleasant greenery of the forest seeming to give way to sinister forms. The trunks here were contorted into unnatural shapes, branches like agony-crippled fingers, leaves more grey than green. Creepers hung in matted coils like serpents, and the ground crunched with the detritus of hollow logs. No life seemed to stir at all.

"Well, we're getting close to *something*, at any rate," Sardâr whispered.

No one replied. For Jack, this wasn't just because he was still annoyed at the elf for his outburst. A deadening silence clung to the air, to the extent that speaking or even breathing felt like an interruption.

Ruth accidently brushed a branch with her sleeve. "What *is* this stuff?" Some sort of whitish-grey powder had rubbed off onto her tunic.

"It's ash," Bál replied, squinting at it. "Definitely ash. But there isn't a volcano around here, is there?"

Then, quite suddenly, the sky opened. They had left behind the canopy of the trees. What they were now standing in could only tenuously be described as a glade. The ground continued downwards to a crater-like basin, stifled by the decomposing remnants of trees. Everything was smothered with the same whitish-grey ash—everything, that is, except the object at the very center of the basin, which the sprite now hovered over.

"What is it?"

Sardâr slid down the slope for a closer look, spraying burnt-out matter about him like some kind of surfer. He knelt and examined the object and then beckoned the others. "It looks like some sort of . . . sword?"

Jack could see what he meant. The object looked like

The Sword in the Stone

it had a handle and a guard, and its blade had been driven deep into a large rock below. The problem was that it was constructed entirely from dead leaves: it looked as if it might crumble to dust if any of them touched it.

"So what's this got to do with the Shard, then?" Dannie asked, her head tilted.

"I think," Sardâr replied slowly, "that this is some kind of protective enchantment. Pulling the sword from the stone would seem to cause an alchemical reaction, revealing the Shard."

"Well, let's get on with it, then," Bál said, grasping the hilt.

The sword didn't crumble away. It didn't budge at all.

The dwarf's cheeks flushed. He tried again, but still it remained resolute. Anchoring his booted feet on top of the rock, he grabbed it underhand by the guard and flexed upwards, his triceps bulging. Nothing.

Jack caught Ruth's eye. They couldn't help smirking. For all his masculine bravado, Bál couldn't seem to lift a leaf off a stone.

This charade continued several more minutes and would have gone on much longer, but Sardâr intervened and suggested he give it a go.

Rather reluctantly, Bál stood back, muttering something about loosening it up for him.

The elf placed two fingers on the hilt and spoke a few syllables under his breath. His fingertips flared with light, but there was no other reaction. More syllables; a different-colored light; nothing. Exhaling slowly, Sardâr stood back and began his signature pacing through the ankle-level cloud of ash.

Ruth gave it her best shot, to no avail.

Jack took up position in front of the blade and focused his mind on pulling power out of the elements around him. The Seventh Shard burst into life around his neck, an ivory beam shooting from the tip to engulf the weapon. After a few seconds it faded, and the sword was left unchanged.

"This is no use," Ruth breathed. "The fairies said only the rightful bearer would be able to release the Shard. I say we head back to the commune and ask them for a bit more detail on what we need to do."

Sardâr nodded wearily and joined her in staggering back up the slope, followed by Bál. Jack was dimly aware of Dannie behind him as he turned and began traipsing back towards the trees. He was halfway up the slope when the girl called out.

"Erm, you lot . . . I think I just did it?"

Jack turned. Dannie still stood at the bottom of the basin. Clutched in both her hands, entirely divorced from the stone, was the sword. Jack looked up the slope at the others. They had all turned too, and their slightly stunned expressions were mirrored in both his own and Dannie's.

There was a noise like a deep breath, and Jack was knocked flat onto the ground. Wind blasted from the basin, throwing ash into the air like a storm cloud. He covered his mouth and kept low, squinting through the grey to glimpse Dannie. He could see her, just. She seemed to have been lifted, the sword in her hands dis-integrating into the whirlwind. Emerald light shone

The Sword in the Stone

outwards from between her palms, illuminating her terrified expression.

The wind ebbed and died. Jack rose, hesitantly, blinking away the dust and dancing lights. The basin had been entirely cleared of ash and dead logs, and he now stood on slightly spongy damp earth. Shoots peered through the dirt here and there, as if suddenly the first moments of spring had arrived. Dannie was back on the ground, next to the stone. The sword was nowhere in sight. Instead, threaded around her neck was a crystal Shard with a tiny leaf symbol carved into it.

Chapter XVI
the third shard

Jack, Ruth, Sardâr, and Bál stood, agape, staring down at Dannie. No one said anything for several seconds. Dannie seemed as stunned as they were—she was looking down at the Third Shard around her neck with a mixture of surprise and alarm.

"Really," Ruth exclaimed, finally, "what are the odds? We pick you up by *accident* in a city we *happen* to pass through, and you turn out to be—"

The ground rumbled. A noise like an explosion ripped through the trees, sending birds spiralling into the sky.

The five of them turned towards the source: back the way they had come, uphill towards the commune. In the space of a heartbeat, they had started sprinting uphill. Darting into the cover of the trees, they headed towards the fairy glade. It was quite unusual, Jack reflected dimly, to be running *towards* an explosion.

Within minutes they had reached the edge of the glade, panting heavily. The surroundings had changed a lot since they'd been gone. Whatever that explosion had been, it had sheared off the tops of trees with scalpel-like precision. The wounded trunks oozed some kind of dark liquid, dripping to the forest floor like black resin.

"Avoid that," Sardâr warned as they slid through the devastation.

They came to the banks marking one of the entrances to the glade. Keeping as low as possible, they edged forward enough to see inside. Jack's first impression was of a student occupation, the fairies huddling together on the grass in the center. His next was of a hostage situation. Black-cloaked Cultists stood around them at regular points, facing inwards like guards in a bank robbery. Beyond them, a colossal metallic form glinted in the sunlight. It was exactly the blueprint they had come across: a metal sphere the diameter of a two-story building, with a sun of Dark energy simmering at its core, supported by four spindly legs. Two more appendages with claws extended from a command box on top, in which another black-cloaked figure reclined. For now, at least, the machine was motionless.

"You've all gone soft!" Nimue cackled. "We needn't have put all the effort into building this thing. There I was, thinking that a pure alchemical attack was bound to fail, but you've all hung up your spell books!"

Jack looked back at Ruth, who was leaning around

134

him to see. He could almost hear her teeth grinding in suppressed rage. He looked back towards the glade and caught sight of something else. The icy slab encasing the frozen elf was there as well, dumped directly below the machine as if it were an egg being protected.

"In all seriousness, though," the Cultist continued, "you *will* give me the location of the Shard and the details of any protective enchantments on it. You might not value your own lives, but . . ." She pulled a lever. There was the noise of something gearing up, and the energy core dilated. Then, with a boom that sent the ground rumbling and branches crashing to the ground, a beam blasted from the machine, obliterating trees in a surge of superheated Dark energy.

Some of the fairies winced, others cried out in anguish, but they all remained seated.

"I will dismantle this forest tree by tree, if necessary, to extract this information from you. Every single lifeform shall be absorbed into the Darkness, and nothing shall ever grow here again. The alchemical infection will spread into the soil and reach across this entire planet. You may be willing to lay down your own lives, but will you pay the price of your whole world?"

Jack blinked. Dannie had leapt to her feet. Sardâr made a grab for her legs, but she was already gone, striding into the glade with the Shard swaying slightly around her neck.

"What's she doing?" Ruth hissed.

The Cultists turned, and Dark alchemy in various forms instantaneously sprung into their hands, ready to stain the patch of ground with Dannie's remains.

The four Apollonians didn't hesitate. In a flash, they were by Dannie's side, Bál grasping his axe, Ruth clutching a rapier in one hand and a spear in the other, Sardâr and Jack crackling with alchemical energy.

The Cultists had broken their circle and were moving into a line, several hands twitching with the instinct to fight. The scene reminded Jack of a Wild West shoot-out, but this was much, much more serious.

"Well, we *did* underestimate you," Nimue drawled from atop the machine. She had stood, her upper body extending out of the command box, and a wreath of black fire intertwined her fingers. "You won't be so lucky this time, I'm afraid."

Dannie's gaze narrowed. "Let them go, and we won't harm you."

Nimue cackled again. "*You* won't harm *us*? Are you mad, girl? We have you outnumbered and, as you would probably say, outgunned." Then, addressing Sardâr: "Is it a regular practice of yours to elevate street urchins to positions of command?"

He didn't reply. He was looking past the Cult to the group on the ground. Jack knew what he was thinking. If the fairies stood up for themselves, the Cult would be the ones who were outnumbered, by a degree of about two to one.

Nimue seemed to notice what he saw. "Oh, they won't be of any use to you. They used to be a lot tougher than this—one perpetual civil war." At his confused expression, her teeth flashed in a malicious grin. "Oh,

The Third Shard

did I not tell you? I'm from around these parts." And her face changed. Her skin, moments before coldly perfect, withered; her flashing eyes regressed to tiny jewels set back into her skull; her sleek hair knotted into willow strands. But this was not a fairy like the ones she held hostage, whose forms were filled with vernal life. Hers was withered like a dying husk.

She looked down at each of them, supremely arrogant, until her gaze fell on the object hanging around Dannie's neck. "You! You have the Shard!" She clapped, and a dark form drifted from behind her. "Morgana, go!"

Black wings unfurled, the raven demon took off from the machine and soared towards Dannie, its eyes phantasmagorical pits, its razor-sharp claws extended to rake the girl's flesh . . .

There was a whip crack, and emerald light exploded outwards from Dannie. It rose, spiralling, extending outwards, forming into a pair of gigantic wings. The kestrel let out a hunting cry and the wings closed on the raven, engulfing it, crushing it within a green tornado. Black smoke escaped as the demon crumbled into nothingness.

Nimue gripped her bark throat, her taut breath the sound of splintering dry wood. Her eyes narrowed into tiny pinpricks, and she leapt from the machine, carried by Dark energy.

the black rose

Dannie crouched and propelled herself off the grass, coming to hover directly opposite the Cultist. An orb of dark flame appeared between Nimue's twig-like fingers, and the battle began.

"The girl has the Shard," a cedar shouted, jumping up.

"Help her! Help them," a birch added, doing the same.

All around the captive group, fairies towered at their full height over their captors. The Cultists tried to back away but found their path outwards barred by four armed Apollonians. Jack smirked and conjured an alchemical sword.

To call what happened a battle would be generous. As Dannie and Nimue flung alchemy between them, the fairies fired spells at the Cultists. They were the most formidable sorcerers Jack had ever seen, adept at drawing on their surroundings to the greatest degree. Vines whiplashed off branches and caught their enemies by the throat; roots wove in and out of legs and clamped feet to the ground; trails of thorns were drawn out almost like hosepipes to bind hands, ankles, and mouths. Against the unleashed forces of nature, the Cultists didn't stand a chance. Within a matter of minutes, all twelve had been restrained.

Jack looked upwards. The sky was alight, the energies of Dannie and Nimue's duel still raging. All the other combatants, whether captured or not, were as far back against the tree line as possible, trying to avoid the fallout. Alchemical blasts ricocheted at an alarming rate, shooting downwards or being hurled into the trees. Jack felt as though he should intervene, but he couldn't risk hitting Dannie instead of Nimue.

A fireball rocketed from the fray to land in the grass beneath the machine. Flames engulfed the grass and stretched upwards, licking at the bottom of the metal sphere and reaching perilously close to the icy slab.

"What are you doing?" Bál had darted out, sprinting beneath the aerial battle to the other side of the glade. A blade of energy arced in the dwarf's direction, and Jack summoned the power of the Seventh Shard. A white barrier spun into existence, refracting the blade into the trees, leaving the dwarf free to chisel the slab with his axe.

Jack jumped forward to help him, but Sardâr caught him and battered him back. Jack followed the elf's gaze upwards.

Dannie had launched a blast of emerald energy at Nimue, which the Cultist had dodged. It whirred onwards, gathering speed, and struck the core of the machine.

The cacophony was so great that Jack instinctively plunged his fingers as far into his ears as possible. The shell convulsed, the thin legs buckling under the weight. The core had ripped itself free of its binding, and Jack now recognized what it was. Identical to the one Iago had conjured back in Thorin Salr, the Dark Eye pulsated with crimson light like a chained star. And just as before, he watched it splinter and release the star's power.

The fabric of reality rent, imploding, drawing all matter around it into Darkness. Nimue tumbled backwards, but Jack could see in Dannie's narrowed gaze her determination to not let the Cultist get away. She was riding on wings of light to keep her steady, and out of the air she drew an alchemical bow and arrow. Notching the arrow, she took aim and fired, piercing Nimue's chest. The Cultist was hurled to the earth with a howl, nailed to the ground, unable to move.

But Jack, Sardâr, and Ruth had stopped watching this. Their attention was drawn to Bál. The dwarf's axe had slipped from his fingers, sucked into the rend. Both he and the slab of ice were being lifted into the air, unable to anchor themselves, being sucked into the Dark portal. The last Jack saw were two faces—one frozen in ice, the other in fear—vanishing into the pit of obsidian energy.

The Third Shard

Chapter XVII
another look in the mirror

With his eyes fixed on the point at which Bál and the frozen girl had disappeared, Jack took several moments to realize green light shone from around Dannie's neck.

"No! Don't!"

But he was too late. A thin beam of emerald light had shot from the end of the Third Shard into the heart of the rend. The Dark energy contorted and then imploded, the portal sealing itself and breaking the link with the Darkness. They were all on one side, and Bál was on the other.

Jack didn't know how he got to Nimue. All he knew was that he was standing over the figure pinned with an alchemical arrow to the ground and was shouting. The Seventh Shard blazed around his neck, and something had appeared in his hand—some kind of club, a blunt instrument, with which he was beating her. Her screams fractured the air as the energy battered her, ripping open the black robes and bruising the bark beneath.

He felt a force pull him backwards, arms wrapped around him. He could hear himself screaming savagely, something like, "Get off! She deserves it!" He struggled against the restraints, trying to beat back at the person holding him.

"Jack! Stop!" Ruth's voice brought him back to reality.

He was breathing heavily. The alchemical club faded from his hand as he slumped backwards, still staring at the Cultist.

Ruth's arms released him.

Sardâr was with them now, alongside Dannie and some of the fairies. They too were gazing down at Nimue with looks not far off hatred.

"Get back," Ruth snapped at Sardâr. "You're even worse. I know what you almost did to Iago back in Thorin Salr!" She stood between Nimue and everyone else. "Don't you see? We're meant to be the *good* ones! If we do just the same—torture, murder, revenge—then tell me how are *we* better than *them*? 'We've got to fight for what's right, but the most important thing is to know when to stop.' Ishmael taught me that. We can't forget it."

The group looked perturbed; Sardâr looked troubled. But Ruth's only answer came in the form of rasping from behind her. It took Jack a moment to realize that Nimue was laughing, coarse air racking her broken body.

"You've got a little moralist here, haven't you? But I'm afraid, girl, the others are right, even if they don't like to think so. Dark and Light, Cult and Apollonians:

we're just two sides of the same coin. You don't have the ethical high ground just because you refuse to kill your captives. That just makes you weak. And weakness yields to strength, *always.*"

Jack had to employ all his self-control to not resume beating the Cultist. Only when a similar fate had befallen Alex had he felt rage like this. And even though Ruth was standing up for Nimue's rights, he could see she was filled with revulsion for the creature below.

Sardâr spoke slowly and as calmly as he could manage. "Where is Bál? Nexus?"

"Good guess, but no. The dwarf and his frozen comrade will be drifting through the Darkness as we speak, cut off from the Light entirely. They will not last long before submitting to the collective force—"

Sardâr turned away in disgust. "If she's to live, then we need to decide what to do with her and her companions. I'm calling a meeting of all the fairies."

Jack was the only one who didn't take part in the discussion. He knew Ruth was there to ensure the death penalty wasn't dealt out, and he presumed Dannie was feeling responsible for closing the portal in the first place. Jack didn't blame her, though. Now that his initial anger had ebbed, he didn't blame anyone. He just sat at the edge of the glade, gazing at the remnants of the machine and the point where Bál had disappeared. He hadn't been particularly close to the dwarf, but the idea of him drifting alone through the Darkness was chilling.

He had been seated for a few minutes when he caught a glimmer of white light to his left. He turned to look and saw a flick of a bushy tail behind a trunk. Ensuring no one was watching him, he got up and made his way into the forest. As he'd expected, hidden behind a large birch was Inari, etched out of the background in ivory light despite the canopy of leaves.

"What took you so long?"

"You've been around people for days. There's been no chance for me to get to you—"

"Why do you need to hide yourself? I *trust* these people. Can't you just—?"

"It's Lucy and the others. The Cult got them."

"What! Where?"

"In the Sveta Mountains. They laid a trap for your friends. They've taken them back to Nexus."

"Why didn't you do anything?"

"You know I can't intervene in your affairs."

"Can't or won't? You gave me the Shard. You woke me inside that volcano. I'm pretty sure you helped me fight that lobster demon the second time, though that's something we haven't discussed yet. Was Isaac right? *Are* you trustworthy?"

The fox was speechless.

Jack waited only a few moments. Then, shaking his head, he turned and marched back into the glade.

The council was dispersing as he got there, and a group made its way to Nimue, still bolted to the ground by Dannie's arrow. Jack walked straight to her, and Ruth quickened her step, evidently worried he would start battering her with alchemy again.

"What do you know about Lucy Goodman?" Jack

bellowed. Part of him thought Nimue looked confused and might actually not know, but he wasn't going to be fooled. He turned to Sardâr. "Get her to reactivate the black mirror."

"Jack, what's wrong?"

"Just do it!"

Sardâr's forehead creased. He reached inside his tunic and pulled out the slender mirror salvaged from the battlefield at Thorin Salr. The back was carved with the rose emblem of the Cult, but the front was glass, which was clouded with smoke like a window on a foggy day. The elf held it down to the fairy.

"She's not going to do this willingly, is she?" Dannie said, apparently pretty sure of the answer already.

"I don't think we need to worry about that," Sardâr said quietly and dropped the mirror onto Nimue's stomach.

The instant it made contact, the etchings flashed indigo and the smoke seemed to unfurl from behind the glass.

"I thought so," Sardâr said. "Automatically activated when any Cultist archbishop touches it. But what's this for?"

Jack didn't reply. He grabbed the mirror from Nimue and took it up in both hands. He could see only his reflection distorted by darkness, but with his fingers pressed to the frame, he felt the strangest sensation of convergence. It was as if his senses had been extended, as if his nerve endings ran through the mirror and out across the universe so that he needed only to focus to see anywhere. He squinted at Lucy, Adâ, Hakim, and Vince. He could picture their faces, as if they were right in front

145

of him, and then they *were* right in front of him, a telescopic image in the center of the screen.

He jumped back, letting go of the mirror. As if suspended by invisible cords, it did not fall. The picture had grown to the screen's full size, and as before in King Thorin's throne room, it expanded beyond the edges of the mirror to shroud the glade in shadows. He and all the other onlookers seemed to be standing in a chamber that was completely black, save for a clinically lit white cube in the center that would have fitted several cars.

Lucy and Hakim were seated, Adâ was apparently asleep, and Vince was leaning against a curved wall, flicking his lighter open and shut restlessly. They all looked considerably worse for wear. All of them were bruised and cut across their hands and faces, and their clothes—Arctic-grade furs over their tunics—were tattered and in some places burnt.

"Lucy! Lucy!" But Jack knew she wouldn't be able to hear him. This was just an image, like live CCTV footage. She and the others didn't have a mirror, so they didn't even know they were being watched.

"Where is this?" Sardâr demanded, leaning to grab Nimue by the shoulder and shake her.

The fairy cackled again. "You guessed right before, just for the wrong question. This room is in Nexus; probably in the Precinct of Despair."

Sardâr dropped Nimue and stood, ashen-faced. He was not looking at any of the watchers. His gaze was fixed upon Adâ, curled upon the ground like a starving cat. He looked as if he was about to reach out and touch

Another Look in the Mirror

her but instead took hold of the mirror and muttered a syllable. In the last moment of brightness before the image was sucked into the glass, Jack thought he saw a tear escape Sardâr's eye and trickle down his angular cheek. But as the natural daylight returned, it was gone.

There was silence. The fairies, from the maple to the cedar, looked aghast. Dannie and Ruth shared a grim expression. Jack could tell what they were thinking, because he was thinking the same. First Bál, and now all four of the other group who had left Thorin Salr had been taken by the Darkness. Their numbers had been sliced to a fraction.

"I think," Sardâr said after a long time, "that we should deal with this fiend. We need a while to think about everything else."

Two fairies passed him and, touching Dannie's arrow to dissolve it into the air, hauled Nimue to her feet between them. She was breathing heavily as they half-marched, half-dragged her over to the edge of the glade. Jack followed, keen to see what was to come of her. They dropped her roughly to the ground directly in front of a tree.

An oak drew up to stand over her at his formidable height. "Nimue, you have a criminal record which stretches back long before the events of today. Most recently the Avalon commune of fairies has charged you with environmental destruction and murder. We have all agreed that these crimes deserve the harshest sentence our custom shall allow. Under the Titania Pact, which ended our last civil war, all violence and corporal punishment have been forbidden. We therefore sentence you to a fate of your own design: imprisonment within this tree until the very end of your lifetime."

Nimue's eyes widened. "No! You cannot! I am an archbishop of the Cult of Dionysus; I cannot be—"

But all were deaf to her protestations.

The oak raised one leafy arm to point directly into the Cultist's face. "Be gone."

The bark of the tree behind Nimue began to ripple as if it were wind-disturbed water. She was pulled back, yanked by a gale that only affected her. She dropped to the grass, clawing at the mud with her twigs, trying to gain some traction, but it was no use. The raven demon appeared from her shadow and beat its wings, trying to escape the fate of its mistress, but in vain. Nimue's body contorted, flicking between many different figures like an early animation film: Lady Osborne in her nightgown, her human shape in a black cloak, several others they had never seen, and back to the gnarled grey of her fairy body.

She shrieked as her feet disappeared into bark, followed by her legs, torso, arms, and finally her head. The raven demon was sucked in after her, and the moment the tip of its ebony beak passed out of sight, the wood froze.

If Jack had never seen that tree before, he wouldn't have thought anything of it. But, with a little imagination, he could just make out the form of a body frozen in time and two tiny jewels positioned like eyes, below a beak and beating wings.

Another Look in the Mirror

Chapter XVIII
the path to nexus

Jack was listless for the rest of the day. He wasn't afflicted by even one of the emotions he thought he should be feeling: shock at Bál's disappearance into the Darkness, anger for the destruction of the forest, hatred for the Cult, savage pleasure at Nimue's suffering, guilt at Lucy's predicament. It was as if all of them were attempting to cram into his mind at once and had halted each other in the process. Above all, he felt tired: in the wake of the day's events, the rest he had managed to recoup aboard *The Golden Turtle* seemed to have dispersed.

Sardâr and Ruth kept their distance from each other and from him, all taking turns pacing, attempting to sleep, or engaging the fairies in conversation. Jack supposed they must be thinking hard about what to do and within a few hours would have their next move planned out to the tiniest detail. He couldn't even begin to think beyond sleep, and yet whenever he lay down he found himself restless.

The fairies had spent several hours deliberating what to do with the remaining Cultists, during which time the sorcerers were held, incapacitated, by various trees and shrubs. Despite their part in the battle, the fairies were resolute in their pacifism.

Eventually, after ungagging and negotiating with a cruel-looking but obviously intimidated follower of Nimue, the fairies agreed that the Cultists would remain imprisoned in the commune until a given time after the Apollonians' departure, when they would be allowed to go free and return to Nexus. Sardâr had begun to interrogate a Cultist but was obviously too ashamed to extract information by force. It quickly became clear that there was nothing to be got out of them.

As the sun dropped below the tree line and darkness fell, Jack went to sit up against a birch at the edge of the glade. Dannie was a few feet away, engaged in lively conversation with several fairies. The fairies seemed utterly unfazed by the trauma of the sorcerous attack. But then, despite the damage to the forest, they had not sustained a single injury among them. Dannie, unlike the other visitors, had also seemed to bounce back immediately.

That made Jack smile slightly. He really liked Dannie. She was fun to be around and always friendly. He hoped she'd come with them and join the Apollonians, not that he knew where they'd next be going.

He closed his eyes and tried to sleep again. An owl

150

welcomed the night somewhere in the trees behind him. The breeze rustled the leaves slightly. Like Dannie and the fairies, the forest seemed to have recovered remarkably quickly from the Cult attack. He could hear the interplay of Welsh and Cockney accents drifting past him on the night air.

"... so what's the deal with this place? How come we never hear of you down in Albion?"

"We've never had very good relations with your sort. There were several hundred years where our people and yours vied for control of the land: our Republic of Avalon against your Kingdom of Albion."

"In the end we agreed to a peace treaty: we would control the forests, and you the plains. That lasted pretty well until the humans started clearing the trees to feed the appetite of their new machines. You think you control them, but which of you is really slave to the other?"

"But why don't you fight back? The forest *needs* to be protected."

"During our last civil war, Nimue was banished for sealing our greatest alchemist, Merlin, inside a tree. You see, that was the irony of her sentence . . ."

"That war ripped us apart. Our society had never seen such horrors. At the end of the fighting, we swore a vow of peace. But now, I think all of us are reconsidering. We fought alongside you because you overcame the Shard's protections. Perhaps violence is justified to protect the good—maybe there is such thing as a just war."

"Yeah, how did I do that? Get the Shard, I mean. What's so special about me?"

And Jack was finally asleep.

He was woken by someone shaking him roughly. Twisting, he tried to pull himself into an upright position. He had slumped against the tree and his upper back and neck were bent into stiffness. He cracked his neck and squinted upwards. It was morning, and the person who had shaken him was silhouetted against the sun. He stood and, seeing the person before him, almost fell back again.

"Dannie! What happened?"

The person before him was still recognizably Dannie. However, superficially, she was almost entirely changed. Her skin was the gnarled bark of a tree, and maple leaves on branches sprouted from her head, shoulders, and forearms. Her factory attire was still on, just, though healthy twigs had ripped through the cloth in several places. It dawned on him that she must have used one of the eggs from *The Golden Turtle* to appear this way. He was beginning to wonder why: her identity didn't need protecting, but her next words cut this thought path clean off.

"I'm a fairy!"

"You're a *what*?"

"A fairy." She grinned at him as if nothing better had ever happened to her than discovering she was actually a tree.

"But . . . but . . ." Jack struggled to marshal his objection. "How can you be a fairy? You've been a human up until now! With *skin* and everything."

"Fairies can change their form, remember? Nimue did it, and this lot do it automatically when they move around. One of my parents, or even both, must have been a fairy. I grew up in Albion looking like a human because everyone else did—I needed to blend in. I think it works like a sort of natural camouflage. And *that's* why I can use this!" She rattled the Shard around her neck.

Jack stared at her, speechless. He felt as if a close friend had just come out of the closet. He wasn't ashamed, just surprised, and struggling to compute the fact that someone who was essentially a plant could be so good at mechanics.

He was brought to his senses by Sardâr and Ruth coming to join them. By their nonchalance he supposed they had already seen Dannie's transformation. They both looked more rested than they had the night before, but they shared the same look of perpetual agitation that must have been clear in his face too.

"We need to talk," Sardâr said, "about what we are going to do."

Jack nodded.

They followed Dannie in sitting down, cross-legged like children, on the grass.

Sardâr exhaled slowly, the other three watching him intently. "We know Adâ, Hakim, Lucy, and Vince are imprisoned in Nexus. And we've got a black mirror which, it seems, the Emperor doesn't know has been reactivated. We have two Shards, as does the Cult, presuming that they took the one from the Sveta Mountains and that Alex is also imprisoned there—and one is in the balance because of Bál's predicament. It seems the two sides are fairly evenly matched."

Sardâr paused, gathering his thoughts. "The Cult would think it suicidal for a small group of Apollonians to mount an espionage mission on Nexus—which is why it just might work. We are not well prepared, but then we could never hope to fight the Cult in an open battle: there are far too few of us. But we may never get another opportunity to finally find Nexus. We can use the mirror to track the world's location and free our friends. We can then regroup, having had an inside look at the enemy's base."

"I guess this goes above and beyond a humanitarian intervention, then?" Ruth commented wryly. "Are you thinking we'd take *The Golden Turtle*?"

"Yes. It's sturdier and stealthier than any of our other dimension ships."

"How many of us?"

"Not so many to attract attention. You, Jack, and I and potentially Gaby or Malik. Remember, once we liberate the others, our group will double in number, so we'll be a lot more noticeable."

Ruth and Jack nodded. Though the prospect of assailing Nexus was daunting, it seemed like the right thing to do. Alex was there, and now Lucy and the others. One of the main reasons he'd joined the Apollonians had been to help rescue Alex: now it seemed they might have a chance.

"So what about you, Dannie? Are you going to stay here with your people or go back and finish off Fred Goodwin?"

"What, you think I'm not coming too?" She grinned.

154

"Goodwin's a tiny fish in a massive lake, and now you're going off to harpoon the whale. You're not shaking *me* off anytime soon!" Dannie's infectious smile spread to the other three.

"You're very welcome to join us," Sardâr replied. "I'm sure we'll sorely need the Third Shard in the coming days."

Their departure was fairly swift. The fairies had spent the day so far assessing the damage to the surrounding forest and working on alchemy to regenerate the trees. It looked like it would be a long job but not beyond their capabilities. The four Apollonians gathered as many of them as possible to tell them of their plans, thanking them for the Third Shard. After Dannie promised to visit at the next opportunity, they left the glade and retraced their route to the river.

Ruth and Dannie strode ahead, discussing the mechanics of *The Golden Turtle*. Jack and Sardâr followed at a slower pace.

"So Dannie's a fairy, then?" Jack broke the awkward silence, acutely aware of their disagreement the previous day.

"It would appear so," the elf replied. "I had my suspicions as soon as she attained the Third Shard. It seems each Shard latches onto a person the same race as that which protects it, perhaps even the same race as the original bearer."

"And she can transform?"

155

"Not *transform*, as such. Merely camouflage. But that's no great surprise." He reached inside his tunic and pulled out one of the golden eggs from *The Golden Turtle*. "We developed this technology from fairy alchemy. I say *developed*; I really mean *stole*. As I've made far too clear, the fairies I've had past contact with haven't been . . ." He swallowed. "I'm sorry about what I said yesterday. It was wrong. I know you expect more of me."

Jack nodded. "That's okay. I forgive you."

They continued in silence for several minutes before Sardâr spoke again. "Jack . . . What you did to Nimue . . ."

"I know it was wrong. I'm sorry—"

"No, I quite sympathize with the emotions. Only . . . did you see *what* you were doing?"

It took a moment for the truth to dawn on Jack. "That . . . that was Dark alchemy, wasn't it?"

Sardâr nodded slowly. "I recognize that it was an exceptional situation, but it would be wise to restrain that side of things in the future. We've seen all too clearly where that path leads . . ."

Jack continued on in silence, troubled. What concerned him most was the knowledge that this hadn't been the first time. He had thought he'd only been that enraged when Alex had been abducted, but now he remembered another occasion: facing the demon inside Mount Fafnir. At that point, he had been lent alchemical strength far beyond his capabilities. Sardâr had put it down to the influence of the Seventh Shard, but now Jack wasn't so sure. It was an emotion his memory most strongly associated with Icarus, Alex's kidnapper.

156

He wasn't sure that, when he and the Cultist inevitably came face-to-face once again, he'd be able to control it.

They reached the riverbank. Ruth must have called ahead, because the golden dome had surfaced and the ramp was already stretched out as a bridge.

Quentin stood next to the hatch. "Jolly good, you fellows made it out of there alive, then?"

"Yeah, cheers for the help, guv'na," Dannie said as she scrambled up the ramp and disappeared down the hatch. "We almost got crushed by a giant spider cannon. Where were you lot?"

Quentin ignored her. "Where, might I ask, is Mister Thorin?"

Sardâr motioned for Quentin to climb down and began to explain what had happened to Bál. Jack followed, leaving only Ruth.

She looked up at the forest, the trees like a bank of glistening emeralds in the morning sun. It was so idyllic here, yet they were about to depart for the place she least wanted to visit. Her nightmares had become more frequent, as if reaching a crescendo before her return to Nexus. She thought she might find some answers there about her past, yet she was afraid what she might discover.

Taking one last sweeping look at the landscape, she clambered down the metal ladder and slammed the hatch shut.

Chapter XIX
the serpent

Alex was sick after using Dark alchemy for the first time. He had fainted and awoken in his bed and spent the following day sliding in and out of uneasy sleep. But worse than the physical sickness was his disgust with himself. He didn't know what was more disturbing: that he had stooped to the Emperor's level or the ease with which he had done so.

His captor visited him a few days later, and they repeated the exercise. Alex had vowed to keep strong and not allow it to happen again, but he sensed in the pit of his stomach that he could not promise this to himself. And it *did* happen again and again and again, every time the Emperor struck out at him and invoked his past against him. Each time, Alex's pretensions to resistance were shattered by a renewal of the anger simmering just below the surface. Something had snapped within him, some control valve, and he felt he had become the conduit for a raging current.

Several training sessions later, all concept of time having evaporated, the Emperor came to Alex and told him they were going elsewhere. Receiving only silence, like so many times before, in response to his protestations to know what was going on, he followed his captor down the steps and out of the Cathedral.

They were on a thin walkway, supported by columns, stretching high above the city to a skyscraper on the other side. Alex had been here before, and with aversion he recognized the Precinct of Despair: the high-security containment facility in which he had first been imprisoned. Was he, after all this, to be thrown back into a cell?

No. They reached the elevators and, after a retinal scan, were admitted to an open-air cube which plunged downwards, far lower than Alex's cell had been, penetrating the deepest parts of the facility, beneath street level, into the rock on which Nexus was suspended.

The lift slowed and stopped, and the doors flashed open with a metallic clang. This was, as far as Alex could tell, the lowest level in the building, perhaps in the entire city. The corridor was lit by the same neon glow as above, with only a single door at the opposite end. As they approached, Alex became aware of echoing screams, which all seemed to emanate from the other side of the door. He shivered.

The Emperor pressed a key on a panel to the right,

The Serpent

and the door slid open. The screams became instantly more pronounced. With trepidation, Alex joined the Emperor on the other side of the door.

The chamber was colossal, perhaps even bigger than the Cathedral. Cells, cubes of about five feet square, were stacked next to and on top of one another to create walls of clinically lit glass stretching as high and as far as he could see. In the wide central aisle, black-cloaked Cultists moved about or floated among cells on levitating platforms. The cacophony of wailing was intense; the prisoners within sounded as if they were being faced with the greatest agony they could possibly endure.

"Who are these people?" Alex whispered, his voice cracking.

"Criminals," the Emperor replied coolly. "Some from Nexus, some from other worlds. Be grateful that you ended up above rather than down here."

The Emperor led him through the main aisle. Alex tried to keep his gaze forward, to make himself deaf to the cries, but he couldn't. In one cell, a man cowered from a huge spiderlike demon that seemed to have already torn off both of his forearms. In another, a woman lay connected to something like a ventilator that seemed to be keeping her alive, but nothing had been done about the blood gushing from her mutilated legs. In a third, a man hammered the glass and howled as a shadowy wormlike thing slithered its way through his empty eye socket and reappeared through his open mouth.

Alex couldn't take it. He fell to his knees and vomited, the shiny bile seeping into the grills of the gangway.

The Emperor doubled back and grabbed him by the scruff of the neck, dragging him to the end of the block of cells and down a corridor to the right.

He was given a moment to recover and he did so, hauling himself up against the wall. He was struggling to find words.

"How? How can you allow this to happen? How could anyone ever *want* this to happen?"

"I am taking you to the man responsible. You will be able to . . . *discuss* these matters with him."

The Emperor yanked him to his feet and continued down the corridor. The blocks of cells were behind them now, and another door was before them. The Emperor pulled it open, ushered Alex inside, and closed it.

The interior was not what Alex had been expecting. With oak-panelled walls, thick carpet, and multicolored jars on shelves, it was more reminiscent of an old apothecary than the office of a prison warden.

A black-cloaked, thick man sat at the large desk, writing, his hood down. His hair was greying, and he had a long, forked beard. Glasses were perched on his crooked nose, and his gaze flicked upwards as they entered. "Ah, so this is the newest recruit," he remarked, standing and moving around the desk to offer his hand to Alex. "Archbishop Faustus. Pleased to finally meet you."

Alex didn't take his hand.

Faustus retracted it slowly. "Your Majesty," he acknowledged, bowing slightly to the figure behind Alex.

"So you're responsible for all this?" Alex said to Faustus, trying to keep his voice as calm and steady as possible.

"Well, yes, I am." Faustus's reply brimmed with badly concealed pride. "Many of my fellows on the Council of Thirteen keep matters moving abroad, but I prefer my work right at the heart of the empire—"

His words were knocked from him as Alex's alchemy flung Faustus across the room. He collided with the shelves, jars shattering and spraying him with colored liquid.

He spluttered and rose, face shining red. "How dare you! Mephistopheles!" With a flick of his hand, a demon rose from a pool of Darkness in the carpet. The immensely tall and skeletally thin figure was clothed like a monk and clasped a spell book. The monk demon raised a bony finger to draw a symbol in the air, but Alex was too quick. In a heartbeat, his signature shruriken was formed between his fingers—not the silvery one he had used his last night on Earth but one seeping with Dark energy. He hurled it, and it scythed the demon's core straight through, the monk vanishing in a plume of black smoke.

Blood blossomed on Faustus's chest, and his breath caught in his throat. Alex conjured several thin black needles that shot across the room and embedded themselves in the Cultist's wrists and ankles, pinning him to the wall.

"Sire, please," Faustus implored, appealing to the Emperor over Alex's head. But the figure behind him remained motionless, watching intently from the doorway.

Alex regarded the pathetic figure before him. The rage was back, stronger than ever before, pumping in his arteries like an addictive drug. He was at one with the shadows in the room, which now seemed to kindle and grow. He felt nothing but hatred for the weak executioner panting with high-pitched pleas.

Faustus became aware of something shifting in the darkness. A shape was twisting its way out of the gloom, slithering across the carpet towards him, tongue flicking from a lipless mouth. It rose above him, tautly balanced on its slender form. He was bedazzled by those emerald eyes—eyes that exactly matched those of its human counterpart behind them. It opened its mouth, knifelike fangs spread impossibly wide.

The serpent struck, and Faustus's screams joined those of his inmates.

The Emperor smiled from the darkness as the last vestiges of the archbishop were consumed. Of course, it had been rather disingenuous of him to suggest Faustus was responsible for this level of the prison. All responsibility fell to the Emperor, personally, as the leader of the Cult. But the aim had been for Mister Steele to summon his first demon, and that aim had been achieved with supreme elegance.

The Serpent

Part IV

"The best lack all conviction, while the worst
Are full of passionate intensity"

"The Second Coming"
W. B. Yeats

Chapter I
the plot

The Emperor of Nexus was seated upon his throne. The vaults of the Cathedral ceiling caught and rebounded the rolling notes of the organ. Candles burnt in banks either side of him, reflecting off the dark stone floor. He could hear, beyond the screen, the echoes of the congregation leaving after the service. His section of the building was deserted, apart from him and the figure now striding towards him up the aisle.

His visitor was, like the rest of their order, swathed in a black cloak. Hood, boots, and gloves left no trace of flesh exposed. Only the sauntering gave a clue whose face was concealed in the shadows: a lithe swagger that suggested either extreme arrogance or madness.

The figure halted at the bottom of the steps and bowed exaggeratedly low. "Your Majesty."

"Lord Icarus," the Emperor acknowledged, tilting his head slightly. "I trust you are well?"

"Quite well, my liege, thank you." Icarus lowered his hood. His hair was sleek and reached his shoulders, framing an aging but handsome face with an inward-curving jawline. The piercing blue eyes scanned their surroundings. "We are alone, I trust?"

"I have instructed the custodians that we are to be disturbed by no one."

"You may reveal yourself, then."

"Indeed." Slate-colored smoke had trailed from the Emperor's skin. His body slumped in the throne, motion-less, the eyes open but dulled. The smoke was projecting from his chest, swirling upwards to form a column in front of the mortal marionette. It resolved into the form of an old man, long haired and bearded, skin and robe entirely grey. The only thing of the Emperor that re-mained were the eyes—twin globes of gold that burnt like suns in a basalt galaxy.

"This vessel is weakening," the grey figure muttered disdainfully, glancing back at the Emperor's carcass. *"These mortal puppets decay so easily."*

His voice still sent Icarus shuddering slightly: it was deep, far deeper than he had thought possible, and car-ried the weight of millennia. "If all goes to plan, then you shall not have to endure it much longer. I trust that is why you've summoned me? Is everything on schedule?"

"Yes, it is. We hold a Shard in addition to the Darkness pour-ing into this world from the Cult's many conquests. The Cultists still believe the Emperor intends to create a superweapon as a

168

means towards greater imperial domination. The real purpose of the Aterosa remains concealed from all but us."

Icarus nodded. "And you think it can work?"

"It is flawless. Ndiuno was the very first world to fall to the Darkness, but I knew at that point it would have to be resurrected once the Cult had run the course of its usefulness. The Fourth Shard still exists there: the Risa Star cannot be reunified without it."

"So your instructions for me have not changed?"

"No. You will be the only inhabitant of this world to survive imminent events."

Icarus grinned, insanity flaring in his eyes. "I look forward to it." He peered past the grey man at the Emperor's body.

"You're right. His body is decaying fast. The skin has turned blue. How is your replacement coming along?"

"Very well. The boy has summoned his first demon and is increasingly proficient at Dark alchemy. As things stand now, he will last me until the end."

"Ironic that an Apollonian will deal the final blow to this pitiful state of the universe—though he can't take all the credit. He's not the first of their number to defect!"

The peals of Icarus's manic laughter joined the organ music, rumbling in the distant vaults of the ceiling.

Jack sat on his bed, staring through the porthole into the gloom. They had been aboard *The Golden Turtle* for at least a week now.

Sardâr had handed the black mirror to one of the crew members on the command deck as soon as they had got on, and it had been linked into the ship's navigation system. It now hung in the center of an isolated oven-like chamber, pulsating with indigo energy. Jack felt uneasy just being in the room with it, as if the intense shadows of the glassy surface veiled unsleeping eyes. As far as possible, he had tried to keep off the command deck and didn't envy those crew members obliged to work there.

Initially, they had passed through murky river water into the vortex of light usually indicating a jump through space. But gradually as the hours had passed, the lights had faded until they were shooting through an apparently endless tunnel. Darkness locked them in on all sides, and if it had not been for the mirror, they would have been utterly lost. It was not a comforting thought that the force guiding them through the shadows was directly linked to the Cult's base of operations.

Jack was restless, more so than he could ever remember. He had tried to recoup some sleep in the first days, but whenever he had closed his eyes, he'd been interrupted by a mental slide show. The last couple of months flicked along the inside of his lids in cinematic fashion: Alex's abduction; Bál disappearing into the abyss; Lucy, wounded and imprisoned, staring hopelessly straight through him . . .

He couldn't sleep, and when he awoke, he felt angry with himself for not being rested. After that, he had taken on as many jobs as possible in an attempt to tire himself out: scrubbing the deck, helping in the kitchen, washing clothes, even learning how to monitor the levels of water pressure. He worked hours upon hours, trying to match the exertion of the Albion factory, yet he still couldn't sleep.

He had barely spoken to Ruth, Sardâr, Dannie, or any of the crew members in the last few days. He might have felt guilty about shutting himself off if he wasn't suspicious the others were in a similar state.

Dannie was as chirpy as always but seemed to have tactfully recognized that Jack didn't want to talk and so had immersed herself, much to Quentin's annoyance, in disassembling and reassembling sections of *The Golden Turtle* to learn exactly what made it work.

Ruth was busy with her captain's duties but, even so, was very quiet. Jack guessed why: she was the only one of them to have seen Nexus; though she didn't remember it, he knew the ghost of her time there haunted her. Knowing that every moment was bringing them closer to her forgotten past couldn't have been easy.

Sardâr, for his part, seemed to have done right by Bál in taking to staying in his room for long periods, emerging sporadically for meals. Jack thought he must be diverting all his attentions to planning for when they reached their destination.

In fact, whilst keeping his body as busy as was possible in a submarine, Jack himself had had plenty of time to think about their plans. The more he had thought about it, the more his initial drive had jaded into anxiety. The mission they had committed them-

171

selves to now seemed like suicide. How could a small group of Apollonians, some of them barely competent alchemists, hope to penetrate the very heart of the Cult's operations? In previous situations—in Birchford, in Thorin Salr, in Albion, and in Avalon—they had only just survived against one of the Cult's Chapters. Now they would face the entire assembled force of Dark alchemists and probably some demons too—and there would be fewer than ten Apollonians. Were they expecting to just stroll in, free the hostages, and be back on board in time for tea?

He blinked. A glimmer of light had appeared on the edge of his vision. He looked away from the brooding Darkness and again into the room. Inari was planted on the carpet staring at him, tails oscillating symmetrically. Neither of them said anything for several moments.

"I'm sorry I snapped at you the other day," Jack put forward when it was clear the fox wasn't going to speak first. "Bál had just . . . and Lucy . . ."

"That's alright. And if it's any better, I'm just as frustrated as you are about my inability to intervene."

"I suppose you can't tell me how I can help?"

"Nope." The fox stretched and hopped up to the bunk, settling on the sheets.

Jack let his head rest against the wall and ran his hand through the fox's fur, scratching him behind the ears. As before, he felt an almost electric tingle when his nerves came into contact with the glowing strands.

"I take it you know where we're going?"

"Yes. You know I can't come with you, don't you?"

The Plot

"I thought so. We're on a suicide mission, aren't we?"

The fox turned his head to look at him. *"I wouldn't put it that strongly. Let's just say your probable life expectancy just got a hell of a lot shorter."*

"We are doing the right thing, though, aren't we? Going in like this?"

Inari scrambled up to sit before him, his paws on either side of Jack's forearm. *"I don't know. I can't tell you what I'd like to, what I'm thinking. No matter what happens in Nexus, certain patterns will become clearer."*

"Patterns? What do you mean?"

There was a knock on the door. Inari nodded at him. Without even the slightest sound, he was gone, the depression in the mattress the only indication he'd ever been there.

"Come in."

The door swung open to reveal Sardâr, long since reverted to his true elf form.

"We're almost there." He paused. "Who were you talking to?"

"No one," Jack replied a little too quickly.

Sardâr looked at him a moment, then shook his head. "We'll be on the command deck. Five minutes."

Jack arrived soon after. His first reaction was not to join the Apollonians at the table but to look toward the chamber where the mirror hung. It was exactly as it had been when he had last been there, wreathed in a veil of purple and black. Again, he felt as if it were watching him.

He pulled his gaze away and went to stand by the table.

Of the three already there, Dannie was the only one

who looked as she had when they had embarked. She had apparently made no attempt to revert to a human disguise. Instead, with her camouflage abilities activated, she now looked something like a space-age robot, her body the composite of the panelled wood and gold around her.

Sardâr and Ruth, by contrast, both looked haggard, shaded with the same look of insomnia and worry.

"So," Sardâr began, rubbing his eyes. "We're approaching our destination. We know Nexus is a city, probably the only inhabited part of the entire planet. Other than that, we know next to nothing about where we're going. I think we can reasonably surmise that, as the Cult is the center of life here, the core of the city will be some kind of church or cathedral. This prison tower, the Precinct of Despair, shouldn't be too far from there."

"What about the others? Gaby and Malik?" Ruth asked.

"They're joining us using a dimension ship," Sardâr said. "We've pulled a couple more agents out of missions on other worlds to assist us."

"So eleven of us, then?"

"Well, that's *almost* a single Chapter compared to the Cult," Jack commented coolly. Having now had his worst suspicions of their operational blindness confirmed, he was significantly less enthusiastic about this mission than previous ones. "So what are we actually going to do once we get there?"

It was Ruth who replied. "Like we said, espionage." She set a wooden box on the table and lifted the lid.

Jack got a look inside. It appeared to him just like a bundle of dark material, until Ruth lifted one out and held it up against her like a dress. "We're going undercover as *Cultists*?"

"It's the safest way," Sardâr replied, pulling the three remaining cloaks out of the box and handing one each to Jack and Dannie. "We took these off the captured Chapter back in Avalon. Quentin's adjusted them to fit each of us."

Jack slid a cloak over his tunic. It was surprisingly comfortable and thick and fitted him well enough. He took the boots and gloves Sardâr handed him and put those on as well. He was now sure that if he put the hood over his face, there could be nothing at all to hint at his identity.

"I'm not sure I like this," he said. "It feels like we're, well, the Cult . . ."

"Have you got a better idea?" Ruth challenged him, her temper evidently as short as his at the moment.

"We're coming up on our target," one of the crew members called out.

"Activate stealth mode," Ruth replied. "And prepare for emergence."

The gloom all around was indeed clearing. Like a black fog, it was furling away from the dome, giving them their first view of the world beyond. Even with the shadows gone, they seemed to have materialized in some sort of alleyway. Dark stone surrounded them on all sides but one, where a side street led elsewhere.

Exhaling slowly, Ruth strode to the glass chamber and keyed something in to a panel. With a hydraulic hiss, the door slid open, and she grabbed the mirror, holding it as far away from herself as possible. "Keep to plan," she said to the crew members. "We're going to be in and out in as short a time as possible. Keep the ship here in stealth mode until we return, and stay inside. Under no circumstances *whatsoever* should you come into contact with the locals here. Is that understood?"

Everyone in the room nodded, and several saluted. Jack couldn't help admiring the fact that, at a time when her nerves must be shredding even more than his, she was able to command the respect and obedience of her crew.

"The priority is to get to the Precinct and back," Sardâr explained as they made their way towards the hatch. "We get the prisoners out and then worry about gathering information."

Dannie climbed the ladder first and hauled open the hatch. As she and Sardâr moved out of the way, Jack got a look at the disc of sky above them. It wasn't promising—obscured by writhing clouds and illuminated by lightning. The churning air was reflected exactly in the mirror in Ruth's hand as droplets of rain began to collect on it. Something from GCSE English came back to him. "Pathetic fallacy."

"What?"

"When the weather reflects the mood."

"I don't know what you mean." Ruth grimaced. "I'm *ecstatic* about being here."

The Plot

Chapter II
the diocese of lord tantalus

Jack got a shock while clambering out of the hatch. *The Golden Turtle*'s stealth mode was very effective—so effective, in fact, that it appeared he was standing in mid-air. "Why don't we use this more often?" he asked Ruth once he had tentatively shuffled to actual ground level.

"Good, isn't it? The problem is it doesn't work in water. The ship's invisible, but water's still displaced: people tend to notice a turtle-shaped vacuum. Mind you, in this weather it might not be so good . . ."

The sky was indeed a matrix of warring clouds, hues of rock clashing high above, sporadically frozen in frames of lightning. Rain extended like a blurred curtain to the ground, droplets forming into miniature tributaries that flowed between the paving beneath their feet.

Stone walls hemmed them in on all sides, with only a single covered alleyway leading to their right. Beyond the walls, towers were alternately silhouetted and illuminated against the sky. It was, Jack thought, exactly the kind of place the Cult would have their headquarters: something like a city-sized concentration camp.

Sardâr raised his hood over his head, and the other three did the same. Nothing now distinguished them from any other members of the Cult. The tallest of the new black cloaks nodded and turned, leading the way down the alley and out onto the main causeway.

They emerged onto a wide avenue. Cubes of clinical neon were suspended from a rail that ran directly above the center of the road, highlighting the panels in harsh blocks of lime. The dark grey buildings rose on either side: their height, thin windows in grids, and extent of erosion identical. Jack saw the towers beyond: dark monoliths at various distances with no pattern of construction discernible. A flash of lightning ripped the sky open, and in that moment he saw the building that dwarfed them all. A gargantuan cathedral, set with stained glass windows and mounted with spires, reached to the heavens. Next to it, connected by a spindly walkway, a single spike plunged upwards into the air.

"I think that's the Precinct of Despair," he whispered, pointing as the lightning faded.

Sardâr produced the mirror and held it up like a map. The surface danced with indigo light. "I think you may be right. Let's go."

"Bit of a melodramatic name, isn't it?" Dannie quipped.

She was ignored. No one was in the mood for humor.

The four black cloaks turned left up the avenue and began walking. The road was curved and seemed to proceed in a wide arc around the center of the city, taking them no closer to the cathedral and prison within. Nevertheless, Sardâr followed the mirror, and although the purple lights meant nothing to Jack, he was sure the elf was able to understand them.

It took him several minutes to realize they were not alone. Figures in groups of no more than two or three skulked along the edges of the street in the shadows of the buildings. It was hard to make them out. At first he thought they must have been Cultists, but then Cultists didn't move like that: they strutted as if they owned wherever they walked. He squinted to his left and right, trying to determine what they were. They were definitely humanoid. They might have been demons, except that he wasn't confronted with the instinctive bile-raising sickness which told him he was in the presence of Darkness. In fact, he got the impression that the figures were purposefully avoiding his gaze, moving along a little more quickly if they saw him looking.

"What do you think they are?" he whispered to the black-cloaked shape the rough build of Ruth.

"I'm not sure." Ruth was looking now too but apparently with similarly little success.

Ahead of them, the line of regular grey blocks was broken by a church, which was about three times as wide as the surrounding buildings and at least twice as tall. It was constructed in the same gothic style as the cathedral, with tall, thin windows and arches and decorated spires set like horns. The cubes of light picked out gargoyles hunched in alcoves, leering with stone malice at the figures trudging inside.

"Look out!" Sardâr hissed.

Jack didn't immediately see what he was referring to, but then his stomach turned at the sight of an *actual* Cultist striding towards them under the alternating light and darkness.

"Brothers! Sisters!" he saluted them, arms spread wide. "You have come to take part in our ceremony?"

None of them seemed to know how to reply, but Jack noticed Sardâr had quickly hidden the mirror in the folds of his cloak. It wouldn't be a good idea, Jack agreed, to look like tourists at this point.

"Actually," Dannie blurted, "we've got urgent business in the Precinct of—"

"Nonsense, nonsense." The Cultist chortled, extending thick fingers to steer Dannie by the shoulder towards the church. "If the business was *really* urgent, you would have travelled through Darkness, would you not?"

"Yes—of course—"

He hailed another Cultist by the doors and marched them to her. Jack and Ruth exchanged panicked glances. It was bad enough that they were being diverted from their mission, but knowing nothing about the Cult's rituals, they would surely be discovered as enemy agents.

The second Cultist nodded as the first explained the situation. "Please follow me." She led them past the trundling line of figures and through the door. As they

The Diocese of Lord Tantalus

passed over the threshold, Jack caught a glimpse of the symbol carved over the door: a black rose, wreathed in thorns, sprouting a spiked Roman numeral.

The inside of the church was cavernous. Columns extended from the entrance to the back; the figures filtered into the worn wooden pews between. The windows and vaulted ceiling were decorated with images of demons and sorcerers, and the far wall was covered by a large fresco depicting a roaring black dragon, wings spread wide and flames belching from its jaws.

"Is this your first time in the Diocese of Archbishop Tantalus?" the female Cultist inquired as she led them up one of the side aisles.

The four of them nodded stiffly.

"I regret to say that Lord Tantalus will not be joining us this evening, as he is engaged in important matters at the Cathedral. Which Chapter do you belong to?"

Jack thought frantically. "Lord Icarus's."

"He is away on a mission, is he not? I thought he would have taken his entire Chapter with him. You are in the process of training acolytes, then?"

"Yes, yes, we are," Sardâr replied quickly. "They are coming along well."

"And so they should, under the guidance of our Lord Emperor and the might of the Dragon. Those chosen to serve must be strong enough to wield the Darkness, must they not?"

The four of them grunted in assent.

They were taken to six high wooden thrones on either side of the fresco, where one Cultist was already seated. Jack sat in the chair uneasily. He didn't like the ease with which they were settling into their roles as Cultists. It made him feel uncomfortable about the supposed difference between the Apollonians and their enemies. After all, they both moved around populated worlds and fought each other there, and no matter the intentions, some casualties couldn't be avoided. And, since he had slipped into using Dark alchemy, he realized another bulwark between the two sides was removed. War, torture, rage—he was starting to see that these occurrences weren't unique to the Cult of Dionysus.

It took several more minutes for the entire congregation to file in and be seated. Opposite him, Dannie was fidgeting and Sardâr's hand was twitching. Ruth, however, seated next to him, was frozen completely still, gripping the arms of the throne, in anxiety. Though he couldn't see under the hood, he got the impression she was staring directly ahead, trying to calm herself.

Finally, with everyone seated and the doors slammed shut, the Cultist who had hailed them took to the front of the podium. He bowed low to the congregation and turned to face the dragon fresco. Then he began his chanting.

Jack very quickly lost track of the service, which the lead Cultist conducted entirely facing away from the congregation. At points, what Jack presumed were acolytes, adorned in tunics rather than full cloaks, interceded with candles and incense. It reminded him of a church service he'd once seen on a school trip. He wondered then, as now, the point of the congregation being there.

In fact, it was the congregation that intrigued him.

Several things were noticeably out of place. Unlike the Cultists, who all appeared European or Middle Eastern, the witnesses looked as if they were from sub-Saharan Africa. Moreover, they all, without exception, looked both impoverished and unhealthy. Every single face staring up at them from the pews was pallid and emaciated, and their clothes were ragged. And what Jack found the most surprising was the deadening silence among the congregation: absolutely no whispering, fidgeting, or creaking of wood. In contrast to the Cultists' swaggering arrogance and affluent elegance, their followers looked beaten down, submissive, and terrified.

The chief Cultist finished his chanting and, with a sweeping swirl of his cloak, turned to the audience. The silence tautened. He spread his arms wide. "Now, to end our prayers, we shall be conducting a test of faith. We shall summon an avatar of our Master to arbitrate the worthiness of our congregation. The clean shall be separated from the unclean, the faithful from the faithless, the goats from the sheep."

He turned again towards the fresco. The two real Cultists stepped down from their thrones and, a little too hurriedly, Jack, Sardâr, and Dannie followed. Ruth remained frozen to her chair.

"Come on," Jack hissed, trying not to attract the attention of the other Cultists.

"Bedazzled by the presence of our Master, is she?" One of the other black cloaks sniggered.

The chief Cultist raised his arms again. The stone slabs between the seven of them blackened and sunk, dissolving into tarry liquid. The pool of Darkness began to bubble, and out of its center rose a spectral shape: an impossibly tall woman, swathed in robes, clasping something that looked like an infant child to its chest. Jack saw its face and felt the familiar nausea. Where eyes should have been there were only pits of shadow, twin pinpricks of crimson light hanging like will-o'-the-wisps in the center.

The dark liquid had not disappeared. It was now oozing down the steps, flowing as down a conduit into the midst of the congregation. The people looked stricken, horrified—but not, Jack realized with a mixture of disgust and rage, surprised. It seemed terrorizing the congregation was nothing new.

The dark liquid oozed under the benches. It was then that the wailing started.

Chapter III
the precinct of despair

An elderly man leapt, screaming, his nails digging into his cheeks. His voice was a hoarse wailing. "I've doubted! I've doubted the truth of the faith."

A woman several rows back stood, eyes set dead ahead. "I've prayed for salvation to a different god!"

A young man, only years older than Jack, writhed and wailed, "I've tried to end my life."

The confessions continued, the air rent by cries. A dozen people, possibly more, were now on their feet, apparently lifted against their will. The Darkness had extended to cover the entire floor in an obsidian sheet.

Jack glanced from the congregation to Dannie to Sardâr. He couldn't make out the elf's expression beneath the hood, but he could see his gloved hands were balled into fists at his sides. He looked back at Ruth. She faced the congregation, her body entirely rigid.

The Darkness had thinned and congealed into netting, an inky web tracing over the slabs, connecting all the standing individuals. Even as Jack watched, the alchemical energy was filtering up their bodies like the contents of a syringe, wrapping them in the web. They collapsed one by one and began moving. Some of them fought it; others seemed too entranced to notice themselves being hauled like baited insects to the front of the church.

He could feel the rage brewing inside him—what he now recognized as the first throes of Dark alchemy. He breathed in heavily and exhaled, trying to keep it under control. He was sickened, but if they were to keep their cover, he couldn't do anything about it. But then, these people were clearly suffering—probably about to be consumed—and could the four of them really stand by and allow that to happen?

There was a flash of ivory light, and the demon imploded in a cloud of black smoke. Silence descended. The captives rolled free; the congregation was stricken; the real Cultists stood frozen. Jack looked around. Dannie's arm was extended, a device something like a Taser crackling in one of her gloved fists.

The head Cultist spun around, his eyes bulging in confusion and rage. He lifted an arm as if to strike Dannie down, but Jack was too fast. In a heartbeat, he had summoned his energy and sliced his incandescent palm in a karate chop into the sorcerer's neck. The Cultist crumpled, unconscious.

The other two turned on them, but Sardâr and Dannie

were ready: the former reflected a dart of energy into an eye; the latter used a diamond of light to shatter through a hastily conjured shield.

When the last real Cultist standing had slumped onto the steps, Jack looked up. The congregants, still appearing as if the pause button had been pressed, stared at them in shock and fear.

How would they explain this to them? Jack couldn't even begin to grasp an answer.

Sardâr spoke in an exaggeratedly imperious tone. "These priests are enemy agents who succeeded in penetrating our home world. The four of us were sent to deal with them for the greater cohesion of our community. Leave now and return to your homes, and be vigilant."

It apparently took a few moments for the message to sink in, and then the first groups of people began to seep out. The ones who'd been entrapped by the demon looked most shaken, eventually picking themselves up with the help of others and shuffling out.

"Why did you say that?" Jack hissed at Sardâr as the doors swung shut.

"We need cover. It's bad enough that we interrupted the ritual, but if we'd revealed ourselves, we'd never have made it out."

"But they wouldn't have told anyone! Did you see how terrified they were? They would have been thankful. Maybe they could have helped us!"

"They may have been terrified, but they've clearly been indoctrinated. Brainwashed. We couldn't trust them."

Jack turned away, rubbing his eyes. He didn't like

how close they had come to allowing a demon to consume people. He knew they needed to retain their cover, but he knew he would find it very difficult if it was at the cost of not intervening to save someone.

Ruth was still motionless, staring at the point where the demon had been. Jack pulled her hood down, checking if she was okay. Her eyes were wide, and she was panting as if she'd been running.

"Are you feeling alright?"

She nodded slowly, not really looking at him. He guided her to a seat and gave her some space. *He* was uneasy, but her reaction was extreme. She'd seen demons before and fought them—this had been nothing new. He wondered whether any of her memory of Nexus was returning to her. She didn't seem able to speak, however, and they had to get on the move again.

After stowing the Cultists' bodies behind a pillar, they crept out of the church in single file and continued up the street. Sardâr had produced the mirror again and strode with head bent, tracing the purple patterns across the screen.

The figures on the fringes—the same sort as those in the congregation—were still there, shuffling in and out of the main neon lighting.

"Who do you think they are?" Jack whispered to Dannie, glancing to either side.

"I'm not sure . . . They don't seem dangerous, do they? They just seem . . ."

"Depressed?"

"Yeah—or *oppressed*."

"Well, who wouldn't be, living here?"

They walked for at least an hour. Lightning continued to rip the sky, intermittently illuminating the clashing structures above. Rain cascaded in a continuous veil, giving the impression of a murky force field hovering above the ground and their cloaks in a vaporous sheen.

Jack soon lost any sense of where they were. They darted down alleyways, through side streets, and back, attempting to negotiate Nexus's labyrinth. The fact that they didn't encounter any other Cultists didn't reassure him but, instead, put him on edge. Even if they had fooled the congregation, the priests would return to consciousness soon enough and alert others to intruders. Though he had faith in Sardâr to guide them to Lucy and the others, he knew their apparent ease of espionage couldn't be put down solely to their skill or the Cult's incompetence. In this world, entirely alien to them, they had no way of telling whether they were being watched.

Then, finally, they turned a corner and the ground fell away before them. Hundreds of feet below, the tightly packed grey buildings spread out, descending into a steeply layered spiral almost like a colossal amphitheater. Out of the center, plunging upwards like a gigantic tombstone, stood the Precinct of Despair: a talon of metal and stone, an architectural impossibility, tapering off to a single column of stone at its base. Set against the storm-rent sky, hundreds of lights pricked holes in the darkness like malevolent eyes. A narrow walkway stretched over the abyss before them, driving diametrically into the side of the tower, a neon-lit door visible at the opposite end.

The four of them stared upwards, the wind ruffling their hoods.

"I'm not the only one bloody terrified, then?" Dannie whispered.

Jack felt as though his insides were gnawing themselves apart.

Sardâr scanned the area and set off down the walkway, followed by Dannie. Jack was about to fall in line, but Ruth grabbed one of his arms. She wasn't looking upwards at the Precinct but down, down into the shantytown of concrete blocks teetering below them. She pointed down to her left.

"It was there," she breathed, her voice barely audible over the wind. "There. I've been there before . . . Jack, I think that was my *house*."

"What?"

"My house. Where I lived. When I was here."

"But that doesn't make any sense! You said you were a *prisoner* here, didn't you?"

She turned to look at him, and her hood blew off her face. Her hair was tossed around in the gale, her face drawn, her eyes set on his, brimming with recognition.

"Everyone's a prisoner here."

Jack stared back at her, trying to comprehend. "But if you *lived* here . . . how did you escape? How did you get on *The Golden Turtle*?"

She shook her head blankly and turned to gaze at the slum below. "I should go down. I need to see what's there."

Jack glanced around. Sardâr and Dannie were drawing farther and farther away from them, their shapes becoming almost indistinguishable from the black mass of the tower. He was very keen to not linger here. If this was indeed the prison—a prison in a city that itself seemed to be one huge concentration camp—then it was bound to have guards. It was only now that he realized Ruth's uncomfortably close resemblance to the people who seemed to exist en masse here. Whether they were religious followers, inmates, workers, or whatever else, he was fairly certain that the Cult would pick up on one in their likeness wearing the sorcerous robes.

"We can't go there now. We need to get Lucy and the others out, remember? That was what the mission was for. When they're safe, maybe we can . . ."

She didn't seem to have heard him.

He tugged one of her arms. "Ruth, *come on.*" Pulling the hood up over her brow, he dragged her onto the walkway. After a few steps, she shrugged him off and followed him to the other side.

They passed below an archway, out of the deafening wind, into a small neon-lit chamber. Four elevator-style doors lined the wall opposite, the rose symbol they now associated with the Cult etched in blue on three and in red on one. A pair of statues—hunched, winged beasts with reptilian heads—gripped the floor with knife-like talons on either side of the doors. Jack shivered as they passed. There was nothing to indicate they were anything other than statues but the recurrent neck-prickling sense that invisible eyes followed them.

"Which door?" Dannie whispered.

Sardâr consulted the mirror once more. The etching

across the surface had changed again, now resembling the digitalized blueprints of a building, recognizable as the Precinct they had just entered. Indigo light pulsated somewhere below, linked by a thin strand to their current floor. "This one." He indicated the rightmost of the three. There seemed to be no controls to get it open.

Dannie bent close to examine it, muttering.

The other two huddled behind Sardâr, fists planted into armpits, cloaks rippling in the wind, from which their alcove afforded little relief. Jack looked over his shoulder. A cross section of Nexus was visible through the gap of the archway—slum housing, the walkway, chapels, towers, and hulking mass of the Cathedral emblazoned against the sky.

He thought about what Ruth had just said. She was right about one thing, at least. Here, there seemed little difference between living normally and being incarcerated. They still had no idea how she had managed to escape the city and eventually be picked up by Ishmael and *The Golden Turtle*, but if Jack had seen the opportunity to escape this place, he would've taken it immediately. This world made him uneasy and not just because he knew what horrors it had spawned. Every moment they spent undercover, he felt they were more complicit in the workings of the Cult. Particularly given the fiasco in the chapel, he now just wanted to find Lucy and the others and get out as quickly as possible.

There was a clanking, and the elevator slid open. The four black cloaks shuffled inside, and it slid shut. They were in an open-top cube of metal, a keypad in one corner. Sardâr consulted the mirror and punched a few keys. There was the sound of air being sucked away, and the cube dropped.

Wind blasted around the shaft, all of their hoods blowing loose. Jack made a grab for his and had it back on within seconds but not before he had glimpsed the faces of his companions. They were all pale and drawn—more so than he thought he'd ever seen them. Even Dannie's usually vibrant complexion had deadened. He imagined he looked much the same. This place was affecting them all.

The elevator slowed to a halt, and two layers of doors slid open. Sardâr stepped out cautiously, the others sticking close behind him. They were in a hallway that curved slightly at both ends, lit with the familiar neon. Lines of doors were set into both walls, each with word and numeral glowing on it. The mirror had changed into a bird's-eye view and was tracing a path to the left.

The area seeming clear, they set off, boots clanking on the metal grill. For the first time since they had arrived, silence had fallen. No hint of the storm outside penetrated these walls. At the back, Jack kept checking over his shoulder. The sense that they were being watched had grown stronger. He had a horrible feeling that something was shifting just out of their sight beyond the curvature of the wall, keeping pace with them, monitoring them.

Sardâr drew to an abrupt halt. They were outside one of the doors on the inner-facing wall. Jack squinted upwards through the gloom to make out the name and number etched into it: Revelation XII.

"Is this it?" Jack muttered, careful not to make too much noise.

"Apparently so," Sardâr replied.

"How do we get in?"

"I'm not sure. Dannie, can you take a look?"

The shortest of the black cloaks stepped closer to the door and began examining it. "This is strange . . . I don't think . . ." She tapped the door, and the numeral dissolved. The rectangles of dark metal parted, and a cube of bright light flashed into view beyond.

Chapter IV
reunion

Alex was dreaming. He was in a flat that had been trashed, furniture overturned and ripped up, grey light filtering through the ravaged curtains. He moved through the rooms: the hallway, the kitchen, into the lounge. A miasma of dust hung in the air, making him cough. A television lay shattered in the corner, crushed by a human-sized picture frame. The picture was an old-fashioned portrait in oil paints: a dark-haired and emerald-eyed young man, entirely naked, a resplendent indigo and obsidian anaconda draped around his shoulders.

Alex blinked. The portrait shimmered. The surface was not the textured swirls of oil, as he had first thought, but the glassy sheen of a mirror. He shifted, and the man in the glass shifted too.

His body felt heavy. He looked down. His pale skin was covered not by clothes but by the weighty meat of ringed coils. A wet tongue, forked at the end, ran in and out of his ear.

He sat straight up in bed, blinking. He was drenched in sweat. It took him several seconds to realize he was not alone.

The Emperor stood by the door, golden eyes luminous in the gloom. "I have something for you."

Alex twisted himself out of the covers and stood up.

The Emperor opened his palm. Cradled within it was the Sixth Shard, the tiny crescent moon symbol glinting in the light from the window.

Alex instinctively felt around his neck. He had noticed it was gone when he'd first arrived in Nexus but had forgotten about it so quickly and completely that he had at no point asked the Emperor to return it.

"It possesses mighty power," he continued as Alex took it and slipped it around his neck. "I thought it might interfere with your training, but I think it can now be applied more profitably."

"So why are you giving it back to me now?"

"Because something monumental is about to happen, and this world will be utterly changed. Tonight you will see a great light in the sky. When you do, you must enter the Darkness, and I will guide you to another world. Do you understand?"

"Yes . . ." Alex replied hesitantly.

There was something different about the Emperor. He couldn't quite make him out in the darkness, but his hands and voice seemed frailer. It was as if his body had sped up its degeneration.

"I think the time has come to show you what I truly am." The Emperor shuffled backwards, right against the door. Grey smoke began to surround him, and like a marionette his body slumped to the wooden floor—all except the golden eyes, which continued to burn in the air like miniature suns. The smoke swirled, resolving into a column extending from floor to ceiling. A figure became discernible: a mountainously tall man with slate skin and cloth, eyes burning with the intensity of a supernova.

The cube hummed with light. Everything else was darkness. As the doors slid fully into the walls, neon streaks sparked from the threshold: tracing a twenty-foot-long walkway from where they stood to the other side, flashed up the surface facing, and dissolved a door-sized rectangle into nothingness. Humanoid shapes, though blurred by the light, could be glimpsed through the gap.

Jack ran, his footsteps reverberating around the chamber. His hood slipped off. "Come on," he called to the others, glancing over his shoulder.

Sardâr and Dannie followed him at a jog, but Ruth was planted to the floor, a black cloak against the neon of the hallway.

It dimly registered with Jack that she was probably having another minor panic attack, but that could be dealt with in a minute. First they had to make absolutely sure Lucy and the others were safe.

His ribs rapped against his lungs, but he didn't stop. The bundle of shadows framed against the light had scrambled up to stand and was now peering into the darkness. The closer he got, the clearer it became: a female form, bristles of a ragged fur coat caught in the glare, russet hair tangled around emaciated cheeks.

He called out to her and saw her back away in shock. He was stumbling through the rectangle. He didn't wait for words or to acknowledge the other three figures clustered around. He flung himself onto Lucy, gripping her as tight as he could.

They stood, wrapped in each other's arms, not speaking, and he had a flashback to a very similar scene on Earth. When he arrived at Apollo Hill, the moment he had stepped into that drawing room and his life had been irrevocably changed, he had held Lucy and known that he would do his utmost to keep them together.

He had failed at that. He had allowed them to be parted. But now they were together again, and he wasn't sure he would ever be able to let her go.

He was aware of Sardâr and Dannie entering the cube behind him; of what must have been first Adâ, then Hakim, then Vince pulled into embraces; of exclamations of surprise and happiness. He could feel his ragged breath mingling with thin streams of tears, the growing dampness around *his* shoulder as well. So little of it seemed to matter, the passage of time irrelevant.

Finally, after what might have been several minutes, they pulled apart and he was struck immediately by how unwell Lucy looked. Her face and hands were frostbitten, bruised, and covered with fresh cuts. She was much thinner than he had ever seen her, even compared to her elf form, and her eyes were sunken in the center of dark rings. She looked like she hadn't slept or eaten in days, if not weeks.

Her expression was one of mixed incomprehension and stunned ecstasy. "How . . . how . . . ?" She seemed unable to form words.

Jack could sympathize. Now that he was here, he suddenly had no idea what to say. "We . . . the black mirror . . . We snuck into Nexus and, well . . ." He gestured at his Cultist attire.

This didn't seem to have cleared anything up.

He looked around the cube. Adâ, Hakim, and Vince stood around them, all looking similarly physically debilitated, though some of their shock seemed to have worn off. Jack was only slightly surprised to find Adâ move forwards and embrace him, to have Vince pull him into a shoulder hug, and to exchange a characteristically wry handshake with Hakim.

"We're . . . we're so pleased to see you . . ." Adâ breathed weakly, an exhausted smiled cracking a scab on the edge of her mouth.

"You know, for people who meant to be clever, you're not very good with words." Dannie was cross-legged on the floor of the cube, using the rare light to inspect and clean a few of her tools. Jack wondered if there was anywhere that she couldn't make herself at home.

"This is Dannie," Jack explained in response to Lucy's confused expression. "We picked her up in Albion." It struck him then just how much he had to tell Lucy, including that they'd found another Shard; and how much she had to tell *him*, like how they'd been captured and whether the Shard they were after had fallen into the Cult's hands.

Sardâr cut through the multitude of Jack's thoughts. "We don't have time for proper introductions. We need to get out of here as soon as possible."

"Where's Ruth?" Adâ asked.

"She's—"

There was rumbling. They all looked downwards. The floor flickered and sparked, flashing in and out of existence as if running on a temperamental circuit. In the moments of vanishing, they could see through to the pit of Darkness below, except that it wasn't just Darkness. Dozens of red pinpricks glinted upwards out of the gloom, flickering like a multitude of crimson bulbs.

For a moment Jack wasn't sure what he was seeing, but then, with an audible gasp, realization hit him like a winding punch to the stomach.

The Darkness blasted upwards through the floor like a wave of oil, a multitude of talons, fangs, wings, tails, spikes, and all other appendages ever conceived to harm. He tried to throw up an alchemical barrier, but nothing happened. He was buffeted upwards, Lucy and the rest of them vanishing in a tidal hurricane of demonic energy. Things were scraping at his flesh, raking the cloak from him. The bile sensation in his throat rose to an unprecedented peak. He was passing away into the shadows, everything fading as he lost consciousness.

Chapter V
remembrance

Ruth ran. She didn't think what she was doing. All she felt in that moment was pure, unmitigated terror of the Darkness present around her as long as she could remember. She sprinted down the corridor, footsteps echoing, cloak flapping, the obsidian mass belching from the open doorway and twisting to pursue her like a raging river. She pelted towards the elevator shaft, hammering on the door. It slid open under her fists and she tumbled inside, pressing herself against the wall.

The doors weren't closing. The Darkness had rolled into view, the froth at the front a surge of forming and dissolving shapes—claws, fangs, wings, spikes, will-o'-the-wisp eyes—a surge of demonic energy reeling towards her. She punched the keypad in desperation, not even looking at the buttons. The Darkness was drawing closer and closer, resolving into a single gigantic hand, extending its grip to enclose her within its grasp.

The doors slammed shut, and the elevator shot downwards. The g-force almost lifted her off her feet as the air was sapped upwards. The shaft was dim but did not possess the same quality of Darkness that had just chased her.

She hit the floor hard as the elevator crunched to a halt, her head slamming into the metal.

She blinked the stars away from her eyes and hauled herself to her feet. The doors had slid open again. This must, she thought, be far below the floor where the others had disappeared. There was no curving hallway of cells here: just a straight corridor, encased in the same neon light, leading to a single door at the end. She glanced up. There was no way she was going back, so the only way was forwards.

She initially thought it was silent down here too, but as she approached the door, she became aware of noises beyond. They sounded like screams, filtered through several walls. She looked back at the elevator. Whatever was beyond this door could not be worse than that ravenous Darkness.

Ruth entered, and she saw what Nexus truly was.

She saw the cubes of tortuously bright light, each occupied by a proclaimed enemy of the state. She heard the endless cries of agony and despair. She tasted the harsh tang of multiple demonic presences, rising inside her throat and charring her nostrils. A screaming woman being thrashed by spiked tentacles; an amputee losing more of his limbs by the second to corrosive smoke; a child, not older than twelve, gasping as the water rose to the ceiling of his cell—a multitude of people, as human as she, were rent both physically and mentally before her eyes.

She didn't make it beyond the stairs. She dropped to the mesh floor, her breaths falling irregularly. Reality seemed suddenly more imminent around her. Another scene crowded into her vision like a hologram mapped onto the first, and the barrier between the present and past was blasted asunder.

She saw the door of her home ripped down in a coil of black smoke: her mother screaming, her father grasping her in his arms and telling her to go. She saw herself running, running beyond the house and felt the heat of it explode in flames behind her. She was running, running into the dark labyrinth of Nexus streets, her ragged clothes rippling in the wind. She was running, running as far away as she could from her home and the torment inflicted on her parents. She was winding down the alleyways, her sense of direction consumed by fear. And there, before her, was a pool of obsidian: a portal from which the cloaked sorcerers always arose and snatched away her friends and neighbors.

And she realized what she had been dreaming for as long as she could remember was not what had happened. She had not been pulled into Darkness against her will, ripped from her homeland through the shadows and

203

emerging in a distant ocean. It had been her choice. She saw again, now, her younger self reach out and touch the Darkness, willing it to take her. Her instinct of terror had given way to all-consuming despair. Now, as then, she had no purpose, and oblivion was beckoning her into its portal.

She raised her head, the lights and shadows of the room swimming together in her vision. She could taste the sulfuric Darkness: the contents of every torture cube not a separate entity but a collective force. She knew it was watching her. She sensed the energies seeping away from the prisoners' broken forms towards the fresh meat. Through the haze, she saw the obsidian congealing before her, slithering down the aisle in an oily pit. Shapes stirred within: coils of serpents, fangs of wolves, wings of bats, demons rising and taking form. A whirlpool of ravenously baying beasts surrounded her.

Ruth closed her eyes and steadied her breathing. She could never fight off this many demons, let alone in her current state. She tried to focus her mind inwards: the brush of the cloak against her skin, the prickling cold on her exposed hands and cheeks, the slowing thumping of her heart. If this was going to be it, then she would depart life meditating on the good parts. Snapshots rose from her memory. Her parents, before they'd been attacked, kissing her good night. Ishmael, brow crinkled with concern, hauling her atop *The Golden Turtle*. The meeting where she'd been appointed captain: Sardâr, Adâ, Gaby, Alex, and other Apollonians positioned around a drawing room on Earth. Jack's apologetic surprise when

204

she'd come across him in the observatory. Jack in front of a fountain in Albion, laughing . . .

The baying had receded slightly, the bile sliding back down her throat. She opened her eyes. The demons were still there, but that was it—they were *still there.* She was seated in a lotus position, and the ground around her legs was humming with ivory light. The writhing wall of Darkness had not advanced beyond the white circle.

She sat and waited, her friends and family with her, the Darkness pressed against her sanctuary.

Jack could hear shuffling: thousands of footsteps echoing through the high vaults of a room. There was some pressure on his chest, making his breathing difficult. He eased his eyes open, pain throbbing through his head. He saw stone slabs, as on a cathedral floor, but quite a distance below him. It took a moment to make sense of his position. He was suspended at least twenty feet above the ground, his torso hunched forwards, his wrists, waist, and ankles clamped to some kind of pole. Wherever he was, it was dim. What seemed to be an immense stage curtain blocked his vision in front. By the candlelight from somewhere behind, he could make out several other figures suspended in a similar position on either side.

"Ruth? Lucy? Sardâr?" His hissing was lost in the brushing of the curtain. None of the figures stirred.

"So we have our first awakening." The voice came from behind him, a low and illustrious drawl.

Jack tried to look over his shoulder but could make nothing out. "Who's there?"

"Blind, so blind."

There was a grinding noise, and the pole he was linked to rotated. He was turned to face the candles, perhaps hundreds, arrayed in a bank stretching to his right and left. Their flickering glow filtered upwards, casting a cave-like luminosity onto the wall behind. Curves and symbols were carved into the stone, and, as his eyes adjusted, the patterns formed into an immense dragon, wings raised above its head, mouth belching a plume of flame. Its claws were planted on the floor where the bank of candles broke; in between them was a throne.

It took Jack even longer to make out the figure there, swathed as he was in a black cloak. Yet there was something different about this Cultist. His robes were laced with a silver thread, which glinted in the candlelight. He was slumped, either in relaxation or exhaustion, but the impenetrable void of the hood was fixed upon Jack.

"You're—you're the Emperor of Nexus, aren't you?"

The figure crossed one leg over the other and folded his arms. "Indeed. This recognition no doubt arises from a glimpse you attained of one of our recent Council meetings. And you—*you* are the elusive Mister Jack Lawson."

"That's right." He assumed, given their captivity, that their cover long since had been blown.

"I must commend you on the audacity of your attempted rescue mission—although such audacity is rarely unaccompanied by some degree of naïve arrogance. Did you really think that you could penetrate this world's defenses undetected? Or did you take our lack of security as a spectacular turn of good fortune? Even before your antics in Lord Tantalus's diocese, the way had been cleared for you to go straight to your friends. Mindless fidelity makes one's actions oh so predictable."

"So kidnapping Lucy and the others—that was just a trap for us?"

"Yes, and you do continue to run into these traps, don't you? Mount Fafnir, the Cave of Lights, now here. If I didn't know better, the ease with which you were captured would make me think you've still got a card to play."

Jack was about to ask about Ruth but stopped himself. If his surreptitious count of the unconscious figures around him was right—and he wasn't sure—then they were one short. Ruth might have managed to get away unnoticed.

"Are we still in the Precinct?"

"No. This, boy, is the Cathedral—the center of our world."

Jack took another glance to his left, towards the figure he was fairly sure was Sardâr. He hadn't the faintest idea of how to get out of this situation, so he had to continue to buy time until one of the others woke up. "What are we doing here?"

The Emperor's laugh echoed upwards and reverberated in the stone. Jack became newly aware of the footsteps, even more tumultuous than before, beyond their current enclosure.

"Oh, you will come to understand that soon enough. In fact"—he paused, listening to the noises beyond—"*very* soon indeed. The final preparations must be made."

The Emperor didn't move from his reclined position. Indigo light began pulsating in the back of his palm, coiling into the shape of a rose, and within seconds his body had vanished into a retreating trail of ebony smoke.

Chapter VI
the aterosa

Jack didn't know how long he was there. He may well have fallen out of consciousness again, such was the entropy in which he found himself. None of the others around him stirred. Once or twice he tried calling out to them but received no response. He wondered if they had been affected by the Darkness that had consumed them in the prison cell.

He remembered the alchemical constriction that had prevented him from fighting back. The same block was present here. Whatever was binding him to his pole, he couldn't shift it, alchemically or otherwise.

It was times like this that he'd become used to Inari bailing him out. Amongst the many anxieties struggling for control inside his head, the nature of the fox's departure factored highly. He was sure what they were about to encounter was linked to whatever had terrified Inari enough to keep him from accompanying them to Nexus.

All the while, he was aware of the growing noise beyond the veil. Echoes suggested they were in a huge room—a sanctuary, if the Emperor had been telling the truth. He tried to nudge the veil, to get a glimpse of what was beyond, but he couldn't reach.

Then, after what could have been hours, the Emperor's voice rang out from somewhere nearby. Hush descended instantly from beyond. A few seconds later, the curtain dropped.

Jack blinked. The chamber was indeed immense: vaults of stone supported by columns and interspersed with stained glass windows. It was crammed to the breaking point with people, well into the thousands, the faces fading into a blur towards the back of the room. The bulk of the congregation were the same dark-skinned denizens as had been in the chapel, but now they were herded in on all sides by Cultists.

Jack was indeed suspended high off the floor, clamped in a *T* shape like a crucifix. Looking to his left and right, he saw the other Apollonians fixed likewise in a line—seven in total, hoisted like war banners in front of the rabble. They were, at last, coming to their senses.

The Emperor spoke from the steps below, his voice resounding through the assembled crowd.

"Brothers, sisters, loyal subjects and followers. You are gathered here this night to witness the dawn of a new era. Darkness has fallen, my friends, upon the age that has passed, and Darkness rises to cloak the new

210

one. All our work, all our struggle against our enemies to purify and protect our glorious realm—that struggle comes to a climax tonight."

The Emperor raised his head, and thousands more glinting eyes shifted upwards to the seven figures suspended in the air.

"You see before you the most recent in a line of heretics who have sought to destroy our city. They have infiltrated with the intention of spreading heathenism amongst us, trying to rend apart our Church."

A swell of noise began at the back and swept forward. The roar of mob rage broke like a wave upon them. The crowd heaved, and several objects were hurled towards the front of the Cathedral, though they all fell short.

"Nevertheless," the Emperor continued, his booming voice prevailing over the riotous wailings of the congregation, "they were unsuccessful. They have been thwarted in their treacherous attempts by the foresight of our mighty Dragon, and they shall be put to use in his service. Subjects and followers, we have never been closer to the presence of the Almighty Dragon than tonight. In his munificence, our great god has shown us the path to him. The Cult of Dionysus has created a medium through which the full force of his power can enter our world. Behold—the Aterosa!"

Darkness rushed downwards, flowing like windswept fog from the ceiling and walls to collect in the gap between the Emperor and the congregation. Something was bubbling black, writhing out of the floor with the noise of a gale. The rose pattern had come to life, its gigantic petals oozing off the marble surface, its thorns cracking like whips as they broke free. An indigo-black mass hauled itself into the air like a huge eye or some unseen deep-sea monster, tendrils hovering about it.

Jack lurched forward and retched. He wasn't the only one to feel the demonic influence. To his right, Sardâr's jaw was clamped shut: to his left, Dannie had lost control and vomited down the front of her tunic.

Complete silence had fallen now. Every pair of eyes in the chamber—whether heavily lidded with fatigue or concealed within the shadows of a hood—fixed upon the floating mass.

"In order to unlock this power," the Emperor continued, "we must all pray. Pray, subjects and followers, for our salvation! Pray for our communion with the Dragon and his Darkness!"

Every single head in the congregation bowed. Only the roll of the storm outside interrupted the reverent silence.

The Emperor lowered his arms and turned to look up at them. With a wave of his hand, he was airborne on a trail of black smoke, hovering at their height. He regarded them each in turn with a malevolent smirk. "Impressed, I assume?"

None of them replied immediately.

This close, Jack saw just how decrepit the Emperor was. His skin was pallid blue. His lips and teeth were cracked—for that matter, so was his skin, fissured like dry mud. What was more, with his every breath, a hint of grey smoke escaped and furled into the air. Only the eyes were truly alive, and they burnt with the intensity of a thousand golden suns. It was as if they were anchors,

212

barely holding together a body that would otherwise have crumbled into dust.

"Well? Are you all speechless? Have you not worked it out yet?"

Jack didn't know what he meant. He watched Sardâr, who usually had the answer to these questions. And, sure enough, it took only a moment for the elf's eyes to close in silent, painful understanding.

"That's why our alchemy is so diminished here. This city, this entire island, is built on haruspex, isn't it?"

The Emperor cackled. "Not just *built* on haruspex—it *is* haruspex. The very buildings are hewn from it—even this Cathedral. It was a gift from the Dragon in all his glory, and with it we have conquered world after world. And now, harnessed into the Aterosa—"

"But we'll all be obliterated! The Dark alchemy surging through the city will act like a lightning rod. This can't be a dawn of your new imperial age if the heart of your empire is ripped apart!"

The Emperor's grin widened. "Oh, Apollonian, I pity you. You cannot possibly conceive of life beyond the mortal. We are about to participate in the ultimate act of collective worship. You and your side pride yourselves on your humanitarianism, your altruism—but tell me, elf, which of us is selfless? Which of us, for the greater cause, is willing to sacrifice ourselves *absolutely*? Behind your façade of charity, your creed is built on self-preservation."

"You're far too precious about your collective Darkness."

"And you are far too precious about your individualism. Which will be remembered: the acts of a few freedom fighters, or a perfectly united world-shattering force? The Aterosa will rend a hole in the Light, through which the Darkness and the Dragon himself can enter unrestrained. We will all perish as tributes to usher in a new age."

"This is monstrous," Sardâr said quietly, raising his head to look directly into the Emperor's eyes. "Do you have any idea how many will die because of this—how many millions of lives will be obliterated by your power games?"

"Of course I do. And if you think you're going to appeal to some humanity in me, you're sadly mistaken. I'm not explaining this to you because you can stop it. I'm explaining it so you know just how much you have failed."

"Are you completely insane?"

The black energy around his feet swirled slightly, and the Emperor propelled forward so that he was only inches from Sardâr.

The elf didn't flinch but held the Emperor's stare.

"Insanity is highly subjective. My ideology is abhorrent to you, so you brand me insane. Your ideology is entirely foolish, so I brand you a heretic. The difference is that I am winning and you are not. Incidentally," he added, looking at the other faces, "do these companions of yours fulfill any function, or do they merely hang around in silence to make you feel supported?"

"Get away from him," Adâ burst out, throwing herself ineffectually against her restraints. "Don't you dare—"

"Calm down, dear."

With a flick of the Emperor's hand, Adâ's voice was muffled, though she continued mouthing furiously.

"Stop that! Release—" Vince's incensed grunts were cut off by the same force.

"Well, they're all going off now, aren't they?" The Emperor swiveled his hand.

Jack felt a pressure close around his throat. He tried to shout but, like the others, was unable to produce a sound.

Sardâr didn't seem to have reacted. He waited, viewing the Emperor's face at close range. His next words were so soft that Jack had to lean in to hear over the wind and murmurings.

"A duel. Single combat. You and I."

The Emperor's mouth cracked into a furry-toothed grin. "And what possible incentive is there for me? I've won. I'm in control. Why would I accept your challenge?"

"Because," Sardâr replied in a barely audible whisper. "I know who the Übermensch is."

The Emperor scrutinized the elf's features. "How do I know you're telling the truth?"

"You'll have to take that risk. If you don't, you may never know and your work will be put on precarious footing. What would happen if, after all this effort, the encroaching Darkness were thwarted because you didn't take the opportunity to deal with the one force which can overcome it? I can't imagine your Dragon will look on you too well then, will he?"

The Emperor's eyes locked with Sardâr's. "Deal. If I defeat you, I extract the information I need. If you defeat me, then . . . ?"

"Then you destroy the Aterosa."

"Rest assured, that will *never* happen." The Emperor

spun and floated downwards from them. His voice boomed again, silencing the murmuring of the congregation. "There has been a change of arrangements. One of the heretics has agreed to duel me. I am to exhibit to him the might of our Lord. No one shall be allowed to intervene. You must all continue praying."

The Cultists began applauding, and a ripple stirred in the main congregation as well. The murmuring resumed.

The bonds clasping Sardâr's wrists and ankles to the pole unraveled. He fell forwards but slowed his descent and came to stand gracefully at the foot of the altar. He looked haggard but intent, the last rags of the Cultist robes clinging to his tunic. He wiped blood-matted hair out of his face and readied himself.

The Emperor descended with his back to the congregation, his robes sweeping the flagons. With a crackle of Dark energy the cloth was rent and reshaped, curling into a barbed breastplate and gauntlets. He raised his fist, and an orb of indigo light surrounded it.

Sardâr took up a sideways stance, and light gleamed around his forearms. The wind howled, the congregation murmured, the Aterosa writhed, the Apollonians hung silently in the air, and the battle began.

Chapter VII
sabotage

Ruth opened her eyes. Something had changed. Her circle of light was still intact, humming with ethereal energy, but it was no longer surrounded by the will-o'-the-wisp eyes. The demons seemed to be melting back into the shadows, dissolving into a single mass of oily blackness on the ground. What was more, the Darkness itself was vanishing, retreating across the floor and up the walls as if into a vacuum.

She looked around. The stacked clinical cubes were still there, but the wailing was diminishing. The demonic presence was being removed from within the cells, one by one, leaving the people inside alone. As if gravity had been partially reversed, the liquid ebony seeped up and disappeared through the ceiling.

Ruth scrambled to her feet, the barrier fading. She

felt suddenly energized. Not only had the strain of maintaining alchemy been lifted, but the air seemed cleaner, as if purged of an infective spore. A groan from somewhere to her left alerted her. She turned to see a man in the corner of his cell doubled over, clasping his stomach.

Ruth knelt, placed a palm on the glass, and whispered to him, "Are you okay?"

The man raised his head slowly. He was a local with a coloring similar to hers. He was the thinnest person she had ever seen. Beneath the shreds of his clothes, his ribs arched out of his torso like the poles of a tent. As he shifted in the light, she saw that he was missing an eye. With the one remaining, he looked upon her face with an expression she couldn't immediately place—it took her a moment to realize that it was mingled shock, terror, and a hint of hope.

"Are you one of them?" he managed eventually, his voice hoarse.

"No," Ruth replied. A lump of emotion collected in her throat, and she tried to swallow it away. "No, I'm here to get you out. Get back."

She stood and shifted her hand higher on the glass. Alchemy flowed much more easily now, and she sent a shock wave through the pane. With a soft boom, a web of cracks spiralled outwards from the point of impact and the glass shattered. She hurried inside and, throwing one of the man's arms around her shoulder, supported him as he limped out of the cell into the main aisle.

His breath was ragged with the exertion of moving just a few feet, so she helped him down to a seated position. She crouched over him, ready to ask where he was in pain.

He feebly waved her away. "We have to get the others out. All of them."

Ruth scanned the aisles of cells. There was indeed a person in every one: some were moving slightly, others weren't at all. The number must have extended into the hundreds, if not thousands. Her brief sense of elation was evaporating into despair. "Who *are* all these people?"

"Prisoners," was the croaking reply. "Enemies of the state, enemies of the Cult, heretics, would-be dissidents."

"So they don't kill you?" Ruth asked distractedly, still gazing down the aisle. "They just keep you here?"

The man spluttered, "Why would they kill us? That would be a relief from . . . from . . ." He looked up and shuddered.

Ruth took stock of the situation. The demons had gone, at least for now. Something had drawn them away. Now that the Darkness wasn't immediately present and she was able to think rationally again, she felt a stab of guilt for leaving her friends behind. They had almost certainly been captured by now, and she had a horrible suspicion that the demons drawn away from *her* were drawing closer to *them*. It had been a mistake to come to Nexus, she now realized. They had all walked unwittingly into a trap.

But then she looked again at the man, who was now coughing up blood. She and the Apollonians could still undo some of the evil of the Cult. If she could free these prisoners and get them safely away from here, then their trip would not have been entirely in vain.

She fumbled inside her cloak and produced her metallic egg. In the flurry of the chase and her remembrance of her last time on Nexus, she had almost forgotten that there were other Apollonians waiting as backup. She intoned a few syllables, and the machinery beneath the casing flared up. She twisted it, and with a slurping sound a bubble of turquoise broke loose, expanding upwards to the size of a dinner platter.

"Command deck."

The bubble fizzed lightly, and as the surface cleared again she found herself looking into the command deck of *The Golden Turtle* from the angle of one of the computer monitors. Quentin, Gaby, Malik, and a pair of other Apollonians stood around the map table.

"Ruth, what happened? You look terrible!" Gaby exclaimed.

"There's a lot to explain and not much time. The others walked into a trap, and they've probably been captured. I managed to get out."

"Where are you now?" Malik urged her. "Have you been detected?"

"I think I'm underground. I'm fairly sure I'm in the Precinct, but on the lowest level. Something weird just happened. There were demons swarming everywhere, but then they all retreated. I think something big is going on upstairs."

"You're quite right there," Quentin replied, his face ashen. "You haven't seen the sky, then?"

Someone evidently had pressed a few keys, because

the bubble fizzed again. Ruth was now looking out the top of the ship. The storm had intensified since they had last been outside, the rain cutting almost horizontally across the air. Lightning flashed more frequently than ever and closer too; it looked like it might actually be striking the fringes of the city. The glare illuminated the mass of the Cathedral, and out of its core a pillar of indigo energy pierced the clouds. Darkness—not just the shadows of the night, but solid, impenetrable obsidian— was collecting around it, swirling downwards like the base of a tornado, as if magnetically conducted.

The view returned to the command deck. Ruth now understood the others' expressions.

"We think that's the Aterosa being activated," Gaby explained. "And if it's their Shards being used to do it, then they're probably in the Cathedral."

"We need a plan," Malik added, quite unnecessarily. No one seemed to be suggesting that they just did nothing.

Ruth closed her eyes for a moment, thinking, trying to block out the other noises from outside. None of the others spoke. Her eyelids flashed open again, and she was ready. "If all the demons are collecting at the Cathedral, then we've got a window of opportunity. I'm not sure what that thing will do, but we know it's a superweapon, so it wouldn't be good to stick around too long. We need to get these prisoners out, and I'll need a hand. Can you lock onto my coordinates?"

One of the crew typed something in. "Done."

"Right, I need you to get over here as quickly as possible—and bring the dimension ship too. There are a *lot* of them. Then we need to get to the Cathedral."

"I thought you were going to say that," Malik commented darkly.

"We need to get the others out of there and, preferably, as many non-Cultists as we can take. Even if it's too late to stop the superweapon, at least we can try and get out of here relatively unscathed."

She surveyed the faces before her. She knew them well enough to see when they were hiding utter terror with steadfast bravery.

As she'd expected, only Quentin's sardonic wit interrupted the silent resolution: "You do know, Captain, that this is a suicide mission?"

For the first time in a long while, Ruth found herself smirking. "Yep. But right now it's a choice between suicide letting the Cult get away with it, or suicide trying to stop them. I know which one I'd rather."

The bubble retracted into the egg, and the light faded.

The ex-prisoner squinted up at her with his single eye, his mouth spread in incredulity. "Who *are* you people?"

Ruth smiled. "We're the Apollonians."

Jack watched with bated breath. Even in their current situation, he had to admit to himself there was something fitting in this. The decades-long conflict between the Apollonians and the Cult of Dionysus had reached its climax in single combat between the two leaders.

He had seen Sardâr fight before—when the elf had taken on and, but for his opponent fleeing, defeated Iago on a floating battlefield above Thorin Salr. He had no doubt about his friend's skill; however, Sardâr was still recovering from the injuries sustained in Albion even before they had been overcome by demons in the Precinct. He must have been weaker than at almost any point in the past.

Moreover, Jack was under no illusions about how formidable an alchemist the Emperor was—the head of the Cult must have honed his powers for years in readiness for such a confrontation. The odds did not weigh in Sardâr's favor.

The orb of indigo around the Emperor's fist suddenly contracted and blasted towards Sardâr. The elf clamped his wrists together and caught it between his knuckles. Rotating it, arms shuddering as if resisting electrocution, he let it fly back at his opponent.

"Good, elf, but not good enough." The Emperor seized the orb in his palm and plunged it to the ground. With an immense crackling, the marble fractured as a shock wave surged across the floor.

Sardâr was hurled into the air. Straining against the alchemical bindings, Jack watched helpless as the elf hit the ground and collapsed.

Sardâr staggered to his feet, crimson streaming from his forehead. He punched the air with both fists, and a barrage of ivory diamonds launched across the chamber.

The Emperor didn't move. He waited until the foremost diamond was inches from his nose, then pursed his lips and blew. A plume of dark flame emanated from his mouth and expanded to absorb the oncoming fragments.

Two horns of fire arched round symmetrically and surged towards the elf on either side. He threw up a barrier, but it was too late. The flames engulfed him, hiding him from Jack's vision.

The front members of the congregation—Cult and others alike—had ceased to pray and were backing away in apprehension. The flames had not quelled with the end of the attack but rose ever higher, growing to consume more of the chamber. Jack could make out the Emperor, striding out of the fire towards the fallen elf.

Jack turned to look at Adâ. She was paler than ever, and a thin stream of tears down her cheek reflected the light of the fire. His horror was heightened by seeing her face. If Sardâr died now, the Emperor wouldn't have to kill Adâ: she would really be dead already.

The Emperor's gloating could be heard above the crackling fire and rumbling storm. "This is over even earlier than I thought it would be. Is this really my opposite, the mighty leader of the Apollonians? I must say, I expected more. This is almost anticlimactic." He extended his hand as if to help Sardâr up, but instead a sabre of Dark energy extended within a hair's breadth of the elf's throat. "Time to talk. Who's the Übermensch?"

Sardâr's words were uttered in a single, ragged breath. "I am."

The Emperor paused in confusion.

That was all the time Sardâr needed. Two blades of

white light blasted from his body. One sliced towards the Emperor, who, recovered from his lapse, dissolved it between his fingers.

"Only one on target, I'm afraid." The Emperor grinned. "Pretty poor . . ."

But Sardâr wasn't looking at him. The elf, along with the rest of the Apollonians, followed the trajectory of the second blade.

The Emperor turned too late, just in time to see it strike directly into the heart of the Aterosa.

Chapter VIII
the end of a world

The bindings around him released. Jack dropped but was almost instantly hurled backwards by the blast from the hovering rose. The substance of the Aterosa had changed. It was no longer floating lazily, its tentacles lacing through the air—it was now twitching violently, as if unable to shake loose the light at its core. The stems flailed as gigantic whips, hammering through stone and stained glass like demolition juggernauts.

Jack hauled himself to his feet and glanced around frantically for the others. He found Dannie some way off to his right, battered against the altar, her skin now the texture of crumbling rock. He stumbled over the growing wreckage and helped her up, sparking an alchemical barrier around the two of them.

"Well, that was close," she breathed. For once, her tone wasn't jovial.

They caught sight of Hakim and Lucy by the dragon statue and, farther away, Adâ and Vince. All of them looked fairly unscathed and had erected similar barriers. Ducking behind the altar to dodge the debris from a tentacle, the two of them darted over to Hakim and Lucy, merging their barriers into one.

The fire had dispersed a little now. Through the gap, they could make out the congregation—or, rather, where the congregation had been. The Cultists were swiftly fleeing via smoke, leaving the nonsorcerous majority to fight their way out. Some kind of riot seemed to be occurring beyond the spasming superweapon: the crowd had rushed to escape via the rear doors. People were screaming, and some were trampled in the surge.

With an immense cracking, the gothic arches were blasted apart. Chunks of stone were carried into the air, exposing a column of energy rising from the Aterosa into the clouds. It was conducting lightning, which now crackled down to claw at the rose itself.

Lucy pointed upwards. Something metallic had flashed by, and a moment later, mechanical flippers descended through a hole in the ceiling. The dome of *The Golden Turtle* came to rest at the side of the chamber, alchemically anchored. The hatch slid open, and Ruth and Malik clambered out. Jack had never been so happy to see them.

Adâ and Vince had joined them now. "Where's Sardâr?"

Jack looked again through the dying flames and

The End of a World

saw them. Sardâr and the Emperor were the only ones standing entirely still. They faced each other before the Aterosa. A barrier of energy stood between them: the meeting point of two forces the exact mirrored equal of one another.

"So this is the way it ends, then?"

"If it ends for me today," the Emperor spat, "it ends for you too. If I am going to oblivion, you are as well."

Sardâr's expression hardened. "If I'm the price to pay for the end of the Cult, so be it."

"Evidently I was wrong. You *do* know the meaning of self-sacrifice."

The Apollonians all acted at the same moment. Eight jets of energy descended upon the Emperor in a furious blaze, Adâ, Hakim, Vince, Ruth, Jack, Lucy, Dannie, and Malik steering them towards their target. They hit him from every angle, and for a millisecond, the light cast him entirely in bright monochrome. Then his body collapsed to the floor.

For a moment, none of them moved or spoke. The Emperor remained motionless. Jack stared at the corpse of their great enemy, not with hatred or even satisfaction but with numb disbelief.

The screams shook them back to reality. The Aterosa had not halted in its self-destruction. Its tendrils still thrashed. Darkness boiled and seeped over the floor like molten tar. The broken bodies of the more unlucky fleers from the congregation were in its path.

"Quick, we have to get them out," Ruth cried, leaping over the side of the ship to haul them up. Jack, Dannie,

Lucy, and Vince ran to assist her. Hakim and Adâ made for Sardâr and helped him limp towards *The Golden Turtle*.

Amongst the churning emotions and thoughts, Jack felt slightly doubtful why they were helping the congregation members, who had been praying for their deaths only minutes before. But those thoughts evaporated in guilt when he saw the first contorted face. A woman, whose leg was twisted under her, looked in terror at the oncoming Darkness. He hoisted her alchemically and jogged to the ship, depositing her in the arms of Quentin, who lifted her aboard.

After they had rescued a dozen this way, Quentin called to Ruth, "That's enough. We need to go!"

"Okay, everyone aboard! Let's get out of here."

The elements of the chamber were distorting now, almost like a surrealist painting. The marble floor contorted into waves that lapped at their feet and threatened to pull them towards the rose. The columns supporting the partially remaining ceiling dissolved into granules, shearing across their path in windblown cones. The curtain that had hidden them before the ritual ascended and fell like a raging bull. The dragon statue behind the altar momentarily came to life, writhing and beating its wings, before it ruptured into pieces and hurtled into the heart of the implosion.

The Apollonians climbed the side of the dome in single file and dropped belowdecks. Jack was at the back of the line, and just before he pulled himself up, he turned round for a final look. The Cathedral was utterly devastated, and plenty more bodies were scattered

The End of a World

around. Demons were beginning to rise out of the inky blackness and feast on the cadavers. Everything without a shield was pulled towards the writhing rose, except the Emperor's body, which remained unmoved.

Something was changing, subtle amongst the chaos but perceptible nevertheless. Grey smoke was trailing out the corpse, weaving upwards to form a tall, slate-colored figure with the same blazing golden eyes. The figure and Jack looked at each other for a moment. Something glinted. An object from the ground flitted into the figure's outstretched hand—a metallic egg from *The Golden Turtle*. Then it was gone, along with the figure, vanishing into nothingness. The Emperor's lifeless body began to scrape along the marble, before being flung upwards and absorbed into the core of Darkness.

"What are you doing, Jack? Come on!"

Jack shook his head and followed Lucy, closing the hatch behind him.

He got a shock when he reached the bottom of the ladder. The corridors were crammed full of the people of Nexus, either crouched or leaning against the walls. He followed Lucy edging down the hallway. The command deck was full too: for once, Quentin hadn't been exaggerating.

They took off and soared through the now nonexistent roof. Nexus sprawled below them. The carnage created by the collapse of the Aterosa had extended well beyond the Cathedral. Houses, lamps, chapels, towers, and all the other infrastructures of the city were being sucked towards the growing core of Darkness. They rose higher, lurching to avoid debris flying in the opposite direction. Several flailing bodies hurtled by, and a large chunk of rock smashed against the transparent dome.

"So what happened to the Aterosa?" Malik asked.

"We managed to sabotage it as it was still forming," Sardâr replied, still leaning on Adâ for support. "I have to say, though, I wasn't expecting it to be this—"

They were all thrown sideways as an airborne house snagged the side of the ship.

"We're not out of this yet," Vince yelled. He had taken up one of the flight monitors; Quentin was in charge of another.

"Were you really going to sacrifice yourself to save everyone?" Jack roared.

Sardâr grimaced and replied at equal volume. "I *was* . . . but I'm still happy you all stepped in there."

Jack's laugh was lost as another house smashed into the hull.

"So what happened to you, then?" he called into Ruth's ear having righted himself.

"It's a long story."

"And who are all these people?"

"That's also a long story. Do you think I could explain when we're not facing imminent death?"

"Fair enough."

A final slab of stone crashed off the top of the ship,

and they were clear of the city. That did nothing to quell Jack's anxiety, however. The Aterosa was ripping apart the planet bit by bit. Before them, the sea had risen into an impossibly high tidal wave, drawn, like everything else, to the center of the Cathedral. The sky swiftly vanished as they hurtled towards the immense wall.

"Are you sure this is a good idea?" Adâ screamed over the increasingly deafening noise of rushing water.

"The only way out is through," Vince yelled. "We're about to test the definition of *submarine*. Everyone, hold on!"

Ruth slipped her hand into Jack's and squeezed. He returned the gesture, his knuckles white.

They were close enough to see the froth.

The Golden Turtle blasted into the tidal wave, and everything went black.

The early summer sunshine warmed the grass of the orchard, and a slight breeze rustled the branches of the trees by the side of the road. A few cars passed, and a dog roamed around the base of some bushes, its owner strolling behind. Two teenage girls in school uniforms sat on the green, their legs outstretched.

"Here they come," Lucy said, nodding ahead. Two figures were strolling towards them: the tall, prematurely muscular figure of Alex and the shorter, skinnier one of Jack.

"Oh God, that kid's tagged along too," the other replied exasperatedly. "I thought this was meant to be just the two of you?"

"We didn't say. And don't be mean."

Her friend gasped dramatically. "Come *on*, Lucy. He just doesn't leave Alex alone. I know they live together, but still . . ."

"He's really sweet. He's a bit shy, but he's really nice once you get to know him. Are you sure you don't want to stick around?"

Her friend got to her feet and, dusting the grass off her skirt, pulled the strap of her bag over her shoulder. "Definitely don't want to now. If you and Alex get close, then I'm going to be left with the other one."

"He's not *the other one*. His name's Jack."

"Whatever." Her friend rolled her eyes and walked towards the road, her bag bobbing at her side.

Lucy composed herself, brushing her fingers through her fringe and smoothing her shirt. In another couple of moments, the boys had reached her. Alex had changed out of his school uniform into a Topman T-shirt and jeans—his hair looked as if it had been recrafted since the morning as well. Jack had remained in his flannel trousers and blazer, tie still on and top button still done up.

They spent the remainder of the afternoon sitting in the orchard. Lucy did most of the talking, with Alex intermittently laughing. Jack barely spoke at all, occupying his time pulling up the grass bit by bit. When the sun dipped over the trees and shadows slipped over the grass, Lucy excused herself on account of dinner. She hugged Alex, said good-bye to Jack, and headed off towards the road.

234

Alex and Jack hung around a little longer. Alex lit a cigarette, the end fizzling orange in the darkness, and Jack had a couple of puffs. He hadn't yet got the hang of it. It took all his effort to not break out into an embarrassing splutter.

"She seems nice," he managed eventually.

Alex nodded noncommittally and stubbed the cigarette out in one of the dirt patches Jack had cleared. The two hauled themselves to their feet.

"Do you think there's anything there?"

"Maybe. By the way, try and talk more when girls are around. They're not monsters."

Jack shrugged as the two of them sauntered back towards the orphanage.

Less than a year later, Alex had disappeared.

Chapter IX
the new world

One day later, *The Golden Turtle* broke into the sunlight.

The impact of the tidal wave had tossed the ship sideways, and a considerable amount of the navigational equipment had gone down. They had been lost in a matrix of water, foam blasting all around them. Vince had piloted them onwards blindly. When it had become clear nothing drastic was about to happen, they had relaxed a little.

The ship was indeed full to the breaking point with refugees from Nexus, many of them wounded. Ruth and Quentin had organized for all the medical resources on board to be brought out and administered, but there were still far too few to go around. Jack had been horrified by some of the injuries: limbs were missing, some people couldn't walk, and in some places such damage had been caused that faces were barely recognizable.

He had seen little of the Apollonians once they had dispersed around the ship. For once, Sardâr's wounds hadn't been the most pressing, so he'd been swept up in the tide of people requiring medical attention. The others had set to work distributing food and blankets and working on the injuries they could manage. To his quiet satisfaction, Jack had managed to mend several broken bones with alchemy and even reset someone's dislocated jaw. He had left the more serious problems to Quentin and the other trained medics.

He had worked in silence mostly. He'd never been good at meeting new people and could not begin to think what he might say to these inhabitants of Nexus who seemed to have almost accidently been picked up.

He'd also been conscious that he still hadn't managed to properly see Lucy, but they both had more pressing matters to attend to, and the mere thought of trying to find her amongst the crowd had been daunting.

There were also far too few cabins for the number of passengers. Jack, like the others, had volunteered to sleep in the corridor, huddled in a blanket on the thin carpet. With the ordinary ship routines suspended because of lack of space, there had been no semblance of day or night. He had awoken several times, trying to find a comfortable position, and lapsed back into uneasy sleep before he'd given up and gone to keep Vince company.

He was on the command deck when they finally broke through the water. They had glimpsed a glow in the distance a few hours earlier and steered towards it. It had grown steadily brighter until their view through the glass dome had been filled with churning waves shot through with amber. Only minutes after shapes had swum into vision beyond, with a frothing that vibrated the ship like a gigantic mobile phone, they burst out of the waves and into bright air.

Jack had to blink several times to check that his eyes were still working. What he saw made so little sense in relation to where they had been. They were soaring through the air, sky expanding upwards and beyond them. The earth was not far below. His instant thought was of a documentary he had once seen about the African savannah: grasslands of yellow and green rolled out below them, shrubs and trees scattered around, blue hills rising into the clouds in the distance. Herds of figures were shifting on the ground—they could have been antelope or something similar.

Jack and Vince exchanged looks of incomprehension.

"I suppose you don't have any more idea of what's going on than I do?"

"Not at all."

The next few minutes were a flurry of activity. As they arrived on deck, each Apollonian's expression changed from identical exhaustion to varied ones of shock. There was no question as to whether or not they would land. All of them were dispatched to spread the word around the ship, whilst Vince piloted *The Golden Turtle* onto the grass. Moments later, they began a mass exodus, the passengers clambering or being hoisted one by one out of the top hatch and to the ground.

Jack's first reaction was that this place and Nexus could not be more different. It was warm—hot, actually—and the air was fresh and unpolluted. From what he could see, the passengers were having a similar reaction. Astounded as they were, he caught his first glimpses of smiles amongst those who had already disembarked. He wondered when any of them had last smiled: something he took for granted almost every day must have been an extreme scarcity in the dark metropolis of Nexus.

It took almost an hour to get everyone off the ship, by which time the sun had risen higher in the sky and the air had become oppressively heavy. As there seemed to be no people or settlements anywhere around them, on Hakim's suggestion they began constructing some shelters.

Even with the aid of alchemy, Jack was still hopeless at this. He had once put up a tent on a camping trip and failed so badly as to not only render his own unusable but also impale someone else's canvas with a metal pole. This wasn't much better.

Adâ located a spot between five trees, and she and Hakim set to work. As gently as possible, they removed the current occupants of the space—what turned out to be several hare-like creatures and something that looked a little too much like an anaconda for Jack's liking. Adâ and Hakim formed a pile of grass between them, arms outstretched, working in tandem. The grass blades rose off the ground in concert. Within minutes, something like a roof had been bound into the top of the trees, rendering an area of precious shade under which everyone took refuge.

Despite their new locale, the rest of the day passed much like the previous one. The medical and food stores on board hadn't been completely exhausted, so the Apollonians, besides Sardâr, continued their work. Jack even chatted with some of the refugees, learning names and lightly speculating about where they might be. Though no one seemed to have the slightest idea what it was or how they'd got there, there was something about this new place that lifted his spirits. For the first time since before they had reached Albion, he was beginning to feel cautiously optimistic about their situation.

It was only when the sun dropped to dye the sky rich ochre and crimson, when the shadows of the trees lengthened and star-scattered blue began to emerge above them, that the Apollonians finished their work for the day and had a chance to talk to each other.

Jack had just collected his allocated meal from *The Golden Turtle* when he heard a cry of happy surprise from the shelter. Craning his neck to see where it had come from, he caught sight of Ruth and an elderly refugee pulling her into an embrace. She appeared as nonplussed as Jack was.

"I thought I knew your face," the man exclaimed, pulling away but maintaining a grip on her shoulder as if she was likely to run off at any moment. "How many years can it have been?"

"I don't think I know . . ." Ruth began, but then trailed off as she clapped her hand to her mouth in recognition. "Hang on, I *do* remember. You were at my parents' house, weren't you?"

241

"Yes," the man replied, tears seeping into the corners of his wrinkled eyes. "Little Ruth, look how much you've grown!"

Still not having any clue what was going on, Jack lost the thread of the conversation. He had just spotted Lucy, who sat with her back against a tree. Brushing the dirt off his trousers to little effect, he shuffled over. She didn't seem to see him until he was very close, and he even had to greet her to shake her out of her reverie.

"How are you doing?"

"Oh, Jack. I'm, I'm okay . . ." She scooted over to make room for him.

He slumped onto the grass next to her. He could tell why she'd chosen this spot: the view clear of the silhouetted *Turtle*, the full fabric of the sky opened out before them across the plains.

Neither of them spoke for a moment, just listening to the noises of the evening savannah.

"Where do you think this place is?" Jack ventured.

"I really don't know."

"Pretty amazing, isn't it?"

"I guess so." Her voice remained flat, and she didn't look at him.

This was very unlike Lucy, he thought, but then, he had not seen her for what must have been about a month now. She had gone to two other worlds in that time and been captured. Snatching a glance at her now, he realized her injuries were not insignificant: bruises and cuts covered her exposed skin, and blood was dried into the back of her tunic. When he had left her back in

242

Thorin Salr, she had been so confident, just finding her feet in a place so unlike her home. That confidence now seemed to have entirely evaporated.

"Is everything okay? Do you want to talk about anything?"

She took a moment to answer him. "No. Not now. Thanks, though." After another pause, she hauled herself to her feet. "I think I'll try and get some sleep."

"Okay, well, good . . ." She was out of earshot before he could finish his sentence.

He remained under the tree, watching the sunset whilst he ate his dinner alone, and allowed his mind to wander.

The last time he could remember doing this was the day all these events had been set in motion: the day he had first glimpsed Inari on the edge of the orchard. He had gone home and sat in his room to eat burnt baked beans. He'd thought he'd been exhausted *then*, but now he really knew the meaning of the word. And yet, though he was concerned about Lucy and the others injured, and though he knew nothing about the world they were in or how they had got there, he felt strangely peaceful. In this state of mental tiredness, he couldn't even begin to start thinking through the implications of what had happened in the last few days. For now, he was just content to relax and let sleep come to him.

The last rays descended over the horizon, leaving a faint amber haze along the line of the distant ground. As though the sun had pulled with it a veiling from the sky, stars began to appear in the dome overhead. Jack had heard that, in entirely uninhabited places with no kind of light pollution, the night sky was like this—and he wasn't disappointed. Thousands if not millions of jewels glimmered in the gloom, arranged in wreaths and plumes of constellations, each one a slightly different brightness to all the others. To describe the night as dark or black would have been a huge simplification: it was alight with subtle shades of blue and purple.

"This is the second time I've caught you stargazing." He didn't have to look up to know it was Ruth. "You're a lot less apologetic this time."

He laughed a little. "There are loads more of them out tonight. Maybe it's just where we are." Then, reminded of the conversation he had overheard, he said, "What did that guy mean about recognizing you? And what was that about your parents?"

"Of course, I haven't had a chance to tell you." She sat beside him in the spot Lucy had been occupying. She explained everything, from leaving the cell where they had all been captured to her sudden remembrance in the Precinct below.

"And that man, Methuselah, knew my parents— knew *me*. He was able to tell me what this means." She rolled up the sleeve on her right arm to expose the lion tattoo furling out from her bicep. "My parents were part of an underground revolutionary organization. They were trying to overthrow the Cult. This was their symbol so they could know who was and wasn't involved."

"But the Cult got them?"

She smiled sadly. "Yep. That's what I remember from before. The Cult broke into our house, but I managed to escape. I think I must have fallen through some kind of portal, because I somehow ended up in the ocean where *The Golden Turtle* picked me up, with my memory gone."

Jack didn't really know what to say. It was a lot to take in for him, let alone for Ruth. "So you're still an orphan, then?"

She broke into a giggle. "Don't worry. I'm not going to desert you on that score. But it *does* mean I can't really think of Ishmael as my dad, now that I remember my real parents."

Jack pondered this for a moment. "I think you can. I mean, you remember your biological parents now, but that doesn't undo what Ishmael did for you. He's still your dad, really, isn't he?"

"I suppose so."

"Have we got any idea where we are yet?"

"I don't know exactly, but I've just spoken to Hakim and he says he's got a theory. He's going to get everyone together for a meeting tomorrow to talk about it and what we do now. We've also got in contact with the other Apollonians. They're going to be here tomorrow too."

"And the Cult?"

"Nothing. No idea what's happened to Nexus, either. Some of the crew have been trying to trace our journey, but we can't make any sense of it. It's literally vanished from all our readings."

Jack nodded. He felt as though he should be contemplating this conundrum, but he was too tired. The night was far from cold, yet Ruth moved a little closer to him. She leaned her head on his shoulder. They sat in silence for a few minutes, hearing only slight rustlings from the undergrowth and the shelter somewhere behind them.

She shifted, and he glanced at her. She had turned her head to look up at him, and at that angle her eyes captured and twinned the myriad starlight. They held each other's gaze a moment longer. Then her eyes closed as their lips pressed together in a kiss.

Chapter X
nduino

It was the following morning, and as far as they knew everyone on the entire planet was clustered in the shelter. Lying, sitting, or standing, depending on each one's injuries, they were arranged in a semicircle around Hakim. The only person not awake and attentive was Sardâr. Amongst all those wounded, only his case had seen no improvement. He was feverish, having lapsed in and out of sleep throughout the previous day and night, and now lay in pale unconsciousness behind Hakim, wrapped in a thin blanket. Standing between Ruth and Adâ near the back of the assembly, Jack couldn't help thinking of a dissection demonstration: Hakim the doctor and Sardâr the unlucky cadaver.

True to Ruth's words, the dimension ships carrying

other Apollonians had arrived just as the sun was coming up. Within half an hour, what seemed to be the whole cohort materialized in a series of light-infused sonic booms sending shock waves through the makeshift camp.

Jack recognized a couple of faces but not all of them: Charles, his wheelchair strapped into one of the cargo areas, and the man who had been on the laptop back on Apollo Hill. He realized that, though he had pledged himself to the Apollonians' cause, he had actually met very few of his fellow agents. There were dozens of them, and he was struck by just how diverse they were: a mixture of humans, elves, and dwarves, and now, with Dannie, a token fairy as well. One notable absence was King Thorin. Jack wondered whether he had heard the news of his nephew Bal's fate and whether this lack of attendance was for that reason.

Combining the new Apollonians, the crew of *The Golden Turtle*, and the survivors from Nexus, their group now numbered well over a hundred. As they huddled together with the sun on the ascendance, it was becoming uncomfortably stifling in the shelter. Nevertheless, they waited, and when Hakim in his teacher-like style cleared his throat, they all fell silent.

"Good morning, everyone. I'd normally thank you all for coming, but in this case the majority of you had very little choice. I'm going to try and answer a few questions in this session, and hopefully afterwards we'll be in a better position to discuss what to do."

Jack caught Ruth's eye, and she smirked. Hakim usually took a backseat whilst Sardâr was the one to give these kinds of explanations. For the first time, Jack could now imagine Hakim in his role as a teacher.

"We're all confused about how we got here—and, for that matter, where *here* actually is. The readings from *The Golden Turtle* have been checked and rechecked, and we made no spatial jump in our last journey. Moreover, those Apollonians who have just arrived had no problem locating us as they would have located any other world. There can be only one solution: this planet *is* Nexus."

There were instant murmurings, and someone actually snorted. Jack looked around in disbelief. The dusty plains, the trees and shrubberies, the sunset in the sapphire sky—he could hardly imagine anywhere less like the stormy metropolis of the Cult's world.

Hakim waited a moment, then asserted himself over the mutterings. "As incredible as this sounds, I have a theory to support it. Jack, Dannie, if you would bring your Shards up here, please."

Not knowing exactly where this was going, Jack complied. He and Dannie stumbled through the seated crowd and handed their crystals over. It only then occurred to Jack how strange it was that they both still had them. He would have thought the first thing the Cult would have done would have been to strip them of these artifacts.

"For those of you who don't already know," Hakim continued, holding up the Shards by their threads from each fist, "these are two of the seven Shards of the Risa Star—the most powerful alchemical objects we know of. The Cult was searching for them to power the Aterosa, which they evidently managed to do by other means. Until now, we've regarded them only as weapons—we've almost ignored the tremendous healing and preserving power they possess. Anyone who has control of one of these has seen his or her life force boosted beyond measure—being able to recover from injuries which would almost certainly have been fatal otherwise. And when the Shards are retracted"—he glanced behind him at Sardâr's unconscious figure—"the user's return to mortal level is very much noticeable."

Jack leaned toward Adâ. "I never got the chance to ask. What happened in the Sveta Mountains? Did you get the Fifth Shard?"

"It's a long story," she replied distractedly, still trying to listen to Hakim, "but no, we didn't. It was gone before either we or the Cult got there."

"But, you may ask, what has all this got to do with the world we're in now? Well, it is my belief that we have so far underestimated the true power of the Shards—we have seen them only in mortal use. What would its limits be if one was fully unleashed? Could it sustain life even for an entire planet under the ocean?"

There were more murmurings at this. Jack was beginning to see where this was going, but the leap in logic Hakim had made was a huge one.

"The Aterosa was sabotaged, and what presumably should have been some kind of cannon or bomb imploded, apparently dragging the entire city and ocean into the Darkness. If I am correct, we are still on the same planet but several thousand miles beneath where

Nexus once was. This world around us"—he raised his arms as if to take in the entire landscape—"was here all along, hidden beneath the waves and maintained by an as yet undiscovered Shard of the Risa Star."

"So what you're suggesting," Charles said slowly, as if trying to make sense of it even as he spoke, "is that there is another Shard of the Risa Star—by a process of deduction, either the Second or the Fourth—that has existed on this planet since before the Cult even arrived. That would suggest some event, some kind of monumental deluge, occurred in this world's past to render it in the state it was in only days ago."

"Exactly. We don't currently know what that was, but we have hope of finding out. The level of life on this world is astounding—not only rudimentary bacteria but beings as complex as plants and animals. This is even more amazing when we consider that all of this has presumably been maintained without the presence of a sun. Given all this, the existence of higher life forms at one time or another is not only possible but probable."

"Sorry, guys," Dannie cut in, "but for us lot who didn't go to school that much . . . or at all, you're basically saying there was a whole world underneath that other one? And there might have been *people* down here too?"

"Sorry for the intellectualism. And, yes, that's essentially it. This is where the majority of you come in." He was now addressing the crowd of refugees, most of them floor-bound with injuries. "I've interviewed a few of you, and it seems the Cult didn't have quite the stranglehold over the population of Nexus that they thought they did.

Many of you were imprisoned for political dissidence, and many more now confess to having had doubts about the government and state religion. For the remainder, I'm sure doubt will come in time. From what we know about the Cult's activities, their existence and reign over Nexus can only have gone back five hundred years at the most—not long enough for legends of a pre-Cult world to have completely died out. Delilah, could you perhaps repeat what you told me yesterday?"

An elderly woman nodded meekly and sat up so the crowd could see her better. She spoke, like the other refugees, in a heavy accent Jack thought sounded like something from central Africa. "My grandmother used to tell me stories when I was a child, stories that she said had been passed down through our family, stories about an ancient people called zöpüta who lived on this land. They had been created by a goddess, who left a divine crystal behind to look after them. But the zöpüta began to fight over its power, and the land was ripped apart by war. Water began to fall from the heavens, and many of the people drowned. Others fled to the mountains, but the waters kept rising. In desperation, the zöpüta prayed, and their prayers were answered. The top of the mountain they had taken refuge in was cleft off and rose into the sky, carrying them far above the ocean." She finished, her voice hoarse from the speech.

Hakim thanked her. "Looking through the obvious embellishments here, this is a very interesting case. It seems quite possible that Nexus and perhaps even the Cult of Dionysus were originally the result of trying to

252

escape a flooding planet. The people in this tale fled to the skies, whilst the healing power of the Shard kept the planet sustained below the waves. If this theory is correct, then the majority of you sitting before me are in fact the descendants of the last inhabitants of this world. You are all zöpüta."

This last pronouncement was greeted by deadened silence. The refugees were glancing at each other, mostly in surprise, but some with expressions that plainly said, *So what?* Jack didn't blame them. As much as he appreciated Hakim's intellect, he wasn't exactly sure what they were supposed to do with this information.

Seconds stretched into minutes. Hakim was beginning to look uncomfortable. He exchanged looks with Charles. "You seem to need time to mull this over. I think all the Apollonians should see to the dimension ships and come back a little later . . ."

It was their first full day on the planet, and it was far too hot to do anything productive. The Apollonians spent the following hours slumped in the shadow of *The Golden Turtle*, stripped down to as few layers as possible. The zöpüta had shuffled into the shelter and were now sitting in a semicircle, not unlike some kind of council or parliament, taking turns to speak. They were too far away to hear, and as the proceedings dragged on, some of the Apollonians retreated belowdecks. Only Jack, Ruth, Dannie, and Hakim were left outside, sagging against the cool metal.

Typically, only Dannie seemed to have the energy to talk. "Dragging on a bit, isn't it?"

"Yes, it is," Hakim affirmed, wiping his brow. "But then it's a lot of information to take in all at once. It's not going to be easy for them, breaking out of the old mindset. They've been locked into the Cult's system their entire lives, barraged with propaganda for generations. Even for the ones who were tortured for questioning it, this will be tough."

While the others moved as little as possible, Dannie kept fidgeting. Since the landing, she had made perhaps her most bizarre transformation yet: sprouting a thin layer of fur and large ears, making her look something like a humanoid desert cat. The changes had now become such a usual occurrence that no one really commented on them.

After a few more minutes of silence, Dannie turned to Ruth. "Shouldn't you be with that lot?"

Ruth blinked at her, then shrugged. "Maybe. I guess I *am* technically zöpütan. I don't really feel like one, though."

"What *do* you feel like?"

She frowned a little. "I don't know. Apollonian, I suppose. I guess I'm sort of a hybrid."

A few more minutes passed. Dannie tried again. "Hey, Jack, your ring's not working."

Jack blinked his sagging lids and looked down at his hand. There didn't seem to be any light glimmering from the symbol, despite the presence of an unknown language. "Maybe the sunlight's too bright to see it."

A few more minutes passed. Dannie shifted several times, crossing her legs, uncrossing them, stretching. "How long are they going to take—?"

"Dannie," Jack and Ruth exclaimed in unison.

"*Alright*, calm down, just trying to make conversation . . ."

The sun had passed its highest point when Jack was finally shaken awake by Hakim. The zöpütan council had dispersed, and several emissaries had made their way out from the shelter's cover to the side of *The Golden Turtle*. The other Apollonians were in the process of exiting the ship to hear the verdict.

A slender woman, whose right leg was supported by a splint, stood before them. Jack noticed she had the same lion tattoo as Ruth's on her forearm. She addressed them in an earnest tone. "We're sorry to keep you waiting for so long. We have had a lot to discuss. Some of us knew each other, some didn't, before today. We will tell you the details, if you would like to hear them, but for now what matters is this: we have decided, as we now find ourselves without a home, to establish a new community on this planet. Our ancestors lived here, it seems, only several hundred years ago, so our society should be able to thrive."

Hakim smiled. "That's what I had hoped."

"And," the woman continued, "we find ourselves greatly indebted to you all. What you have done for us is nothing less than an act of selfless heroism. And yet, there is so little we know about you. Where do you come from? How is it you were in Nexus and can speak our language so well? We would be honored if you would share a meal with us this evening."

Hakim's smile widened, and he actually embraced the woman. She looked disorientated but not unhappy.

As Jack watched, he felt Ruth's hand slip into his and squeeze lightly.

Chapter XI
the übermensch

It was only that evening that Jack realized he'd actually never been to a party before. It had used to bother him that Lucy was invited to all the gatherings when he never was, but after that evening, he couldn't imagine how a group of teenagers drinking in someone's living room could possibly match up to what they had been treated to.

They'd spent the rest of the afternoon inside *The Golden Turtle*, sorting out the stocks of provisions and clearing out anything left behind. When they emerged, night had fallen and flickering lights were emanating from the shelter. As they moved closer, it was clear that the zöpüta had been hard at work. The canopy had been extended over more trees, now with something like walls, and the main area had been set out like a giant buffet. Smoky aromas wafted towards them, and Jack felt his stomach rumble. The lights were a series of fires licking an assortment of vegetables and something that probably used to be one of the antelope creatures.

The Apollonians had places reserved around the circle, equally dispersed amongst the zöpüta. Jack sunk into a cross-legged position between a sinewy man and a grandmotherly figure. They ate with their hands out of bowls crafted from something like coconut shells. The food was delicious: Jack couldn't remember tasting anything as good. After the soot-encrusted meals of Albion and the adequate but minimal rations from *The Golden Turtle*, it was refreshing to taste something properly organic. Dannie devoured hers within minutes and made straight for second helpings. Only after a fourth or fifth course did Jack put down his bowl, in recognition that his stomach would mutiny if forced to take any more in.

The shelter bubbled with conversation throughout the meal. Jack got talking to the man next to him, who had been among the congregation in the Cathedral. Jack's initial reservations about the man's complicity in the Cult's rule vanished immediately when he learnt that his wife and daughter had been lost in the cataclysm. Jack tried to ease the conversation to a less distressing topic, and they were soon talking about the new world.

The old woman, meanwhile, wanted to know everything about him and the other Apollonians. Feeling a little as if he was telling his life story, Jack explained about Earth, the Cult's attack, meeting the Apollonians, and everything they'd seen and done since then. All the while she nodded, occasionally volunteering a question

258

or asking him to point someone out around the circle. It was only when he got to the bit about Thorin Salr that he remembered Adâ's caution to them not to tell any locals about who they truly were. But then, he thought, this must be an exception. These people had seen enough to know there was something beyond their closeted world.

The only Apollonian who looked uncomfortable was Lucy. She sat next to a girl of a similar age, and though the zöpüta kept trying to engage her in conversation, she gave only single-word answers before turning back to her bowl.

Jack assumed the meal would be the end of the evening, but he was completely wrong. Once the last morsels of meat had been scraped off the bones and the vegetables had been devoured entirely, the remnants were cleared away. People started getting to their feet, and Jack followed, not entirely sure what he was meant to be doing. Then, shakily at first but with growing confidence, a drumbeat rose. Another followed at a slightly different rhythm and another, and then came the rattling of some other percussion instrument.

The zöpüta began to shuffle, a little awkwardly to begin with, but with growing confidence. Several broke out into the middle of the circle, tossing their heads back and jumping from one foot to the other. As the beat continued, the group joined in the communal dance.

Jack remained where he was. The man to Jack's right had been pulled in by a friend.

The old woman squinted at Jack. "Well, if you're not going, I am." And she jigged creakily from foot to foot into the crowd.

259

He looked around for the other Apollonians. Many of them had joined in, though a small group had collected around Charles, either to keep him company or as an excuse not to dance. Jack made his way over.

Hakim shimmied past, accompanied by the emissary from earlier in the day. "I knew the Cult didn't have complete control, but I was *not* expecting this!"

"We have a strong tradition of underground music," the emissary replied over the beat. "Of course, our instruments were destroyed, but we managed to cobble some imitations together this afternoon."

"Very impressive!"

"Not a dancer then, Jack?" Charles smirked, tapping the rhythm on the arm of his wheelchair. "You should make the most of it. I'd be out there if I could."

Jack smiled sheepishly and took up a token foot tapping.

Adâ was part of the nondancing group, her face reflecting the intermittent firelight as bodies swooped in front of the flames. She wasn't smiling or even moving at all to the rhythm. With an odd stab of reminiscence, Jack thought of the first time he had met her. She had been extremely tense then, concerned about Sardâr's well-being, and that had manifested itself as cold impatience. He got a sense of the same tension now.

"How's Sardâr?" he ventured, making sure only she could hear him.

Adâ exhaled slowly. "He's . . . sleeping. That fight with the Emperor took its toll badly, on top of the other recent injuries."

"But he's going to get better, isn't—?"

Ruth burst out of the rippling circle, her face flushed. "Aren't you joining in?" she addressed Jack, panting.

He glanced distractedly at Adâ, but she shook her head. "I don't dance," he said.

"What do you mean you *don't dance*?" Ruth tugged at his wrist, and his resistance gave way. She pulled him into the midst of the crowd and began to move her body with the beat.

Jack stood awkwardly, unsure of what to do. He was very conscious of being the only person in the entire crowd not dancing.

"Come on." Ruth grinned. "If you really can't, I'll show you how."

She placed her hands on his hips and pulled him closer, rolling him in time with her own motion. He moved his hands to her waist, and they drew nearer still. The flames reflected concave in her eyes. Her breath was warm on his cheek. Then they were kissing.

"I thought so," Vince called, moving past them with his arms around a zöpütan woman.

Jack and Ruth both laughed, a little abashed.

"No, by all means, carry on," Vince added and disappeared into the mesh of people.

The next few days were hard but rewarding work. After everything from the celebration night had been cleared away, the zöpütan council reconvened and several hours later came out with a resolution. They were going to establish a community on this new world, naming it Nduino after the revolutionary cell for which Ruth's parents and many others had laid down their lives. They were going to hold a series of further meetings to draw up a charter of laws so that they could live in greatest possible harmony with each other and this new environment. In the meantime, they would begin extending the shelters in the most sustainable way possible.

The Apollonians found themselves in an odd position. For the first time since their foundation, they had no enemy to fight, no cataclysm to prevent or plan for, no definite purpose to fulfill. It seemed natural that they should, for the time being, help build up Nduino. With Charles acting as architect, they all pitched in collecting materials, crafting them and meshing them together, putting up canopies and constructing rudimentary huts. It was tiring, and in the superheated middle of the day they took prolonged breaks under one of the canopies. However, with every new structure erected came a growing sense of progress.

There was only one thing that marred their time there. All of the refugees, however shakily and sporadically, were getting gradually better. The same could not be said for Sardâr. The elf had been lapsing in and out of consciousness their entire time on Nduino, and Adâ had attended him almost constantly. Apparently feverish, he'd been moved aboard to rest in the cool environment of *The Golden Turtle*.

The others had offered to keep vigil, but Adâ remained resolute. She said he was her responsibility and the others should assist the zöpüta in building their community. Jack had seen nothing of Sardâr since he'd been moved inside and very little of Adâ. Whenever she climbed down the side of the ship or made a run for water, she looked increasingly worn down.

To a lesser extent, this also affected Hakim. Whilst he was sure to keep up an optimistic front as the de facto leader of the Apollonians, Hakim was sinking, and it was increasingly apparent to Jack in moments of inaction. When Hakim got away from the work periodically to drop down the hatch of the ship, he always returned more restrained than before.

A group had just erected another miniature shelter when Jack caught sight of Adâ emerging from the ship. Hakim stood next to Jack, looking in the same direction.

"They seem really close."

Hakim smiled slightly. "They always were. I've never seen a couple quite like those two."

"How long have they been together?"

"Years and years. They went to school together, to university. That's where I met both of them. I've never known either of them to be with anyone else. They both had successful careers, one as a teacher, one as a lawyer, but they've never parted . . ." He trailed off.

Jack had an uncomfortable feeling that Hakim had been about to say, *Until now.* "He's not doing well, is he?"

Hakim took a moment to reply. "No, he's not."

"Why's he been affected so much worse than the others?" Jack pressed, hoping he wasn't sounding too insensitive.

"That's the problem—we don't know exactly what's

wrong with him. He was weak already, from all the events in Thorin Salr and Albion, and the duel with the Emperor seems to have tipped him over the edge. The others injured may have been tortured or caught in the wreckage, but none of them had to face off with possibly the most powerful alchemist of our era. And then there's the matter I spoke about at the meeting. Using a Shard for too long means you become accustomed to it: the power becomes natural to you. When it's gone, your idea of your limits is . . . warped."

Jack didn't reply. His gaze followed Adâ, who had sunk to crouch in the shadow of the ship.

"Should we go and talk to her?"

"I've tried. So have Charles and Vince and others too. There's nothing any of us can say that will make the situation any better. It's a waiting game now."

Later that day, Jack finally got the chance to see Sardâr. Adâ had appeared at his side as he had been tying some leaves together and told him that Sardâr wanted to speak to him. Hurriedly leaving what he was doing, he followed her into the ship and down one of the corridors. She slid open a cabin door and muttered a few words, then stood aside to let him in, closing the door behind her.

The room was dimly lit, the amber glow from the lamp shivering slightly against the opposite wall. It took a moment for Jack to realize that the lump of shadows on the bed was Sardâr—his only movement was the hint of his chest rising and falling.

"Come closer, Jack." His voice was barely audible,

rasping like the rustle of leafless branches.

Jack moved up to the bed. He was about to ask "Are you alright?" but the sight he was met with answered the question all too clearly for him. He had never seen anyone look so weak. The elf's face seemed to have collapsed on itself, the lamplight shadowing the deep recesses of cheeks and eye sockets. His hair had thinned and greyed, and his hands, laid upon his stomach, looked skeletal. What appeared to be life-support aids only exacerbated the dreary effect. Sardâr looked as if he was caught in a cradle of wires, weaving over and between the blankets and puncturing his skin. Jack involuntarily raised his hand to his mouth, then forcibly lowered it. He had no idea what to say.

Sardâr gathered his energy, then spoke again. "There's something I need to tell you."

"Can't this wait until you're better?"

The elf smiled sadly. "I'm not sure that's going to happen. This can't wait."

Jack paused, then nodded.

"Good. Now take off your language ring."

Puzzled, Jack struggled to pull the ring off his finger. It had been on for so long that it left a red welt against his knuckle. As before, the symbol wasn't lit up.

"Now is there anything different?"

"No," Jack replied slowly. "Wait. You're speaking your language, aren't you? How can I understand you?"

Sardâr closed his eyes and breathed out slowly. "Just as I thought. It hasn't worked in a while, has it?"

Jack thought for a moment. "No, I suppose not. Dannie pointed it out to me the other day, but even before then . . . What does it mean?"

Sardâr didn't reply, his eyes still closed.

"Sardâr, *what does it mean?*"

The elf's next words were so faint that Jack had to lean in until he could feel the breath on his cheek.

"It means that you are the Übermensch."

Chapter XII
departures

Sardâr died the following day.

Looking back on it, Jack remembered thinking there should have been a thunderstorm or some other seismic event. There wasn't. There was just Adâ, emerging from the ship looking wrecked, the first Apollonians halting their activities, realizing what had happened, clustering about her, followed by more and more people. Jack stayed out of it, feeling like a pebble as people streamed by. Her sobs were muffled by the amassed bodies.

The rest of that day was a blur. No more work was done. The body was conveyed off the ship in the most respectful way possible. It had been wrapped in one of Sardâr's old cloaks. It wasn't *actually* Sardâr under there; it couldn't be. At least, for the time being, Jack could pretend it wasn't. The folds of brown under the sun could have been disguising anyone.

A pyre was formed in an open space beyond the shelters. No one questioned this—it seemed that Adâ, along with several others, had known of his preference. It was a mound of bark, grass, and dry leaves, into which the cloaked shape was placed like a cradle. Then they dispersed, waiting for nightfall.

Sometime afterwards—he had no idea how long—Jack found himself slumped in the shadow of *The Golden Turtle*, hidden from sight of the shelters. A glimmer of white sprung up next to him. Inari sat on his hind legs, the thick, paintbrush-like tails wafting. For once, he didn't speak, considering Jack with his beady black eyes.

Jack didn't acknowledge him immediately but maintained his gaze over the savannah. He didn't want to talk, especially about what had just happened, but one thing had just become clear. "You knew, didn't you?"

"That you're the Übermensch? Yes."

"I suppose it's pointless asking why you didn't tell me."

"For the same reason I can't tell you everything right now. I'm constrained—"

"But by who?" Jack stomped the dirt with one foot. "The Cult's gone! The Emperor's gone! Even Sardâr"—the words caught in his throat, but he forged ahead—"even Sardâr's gone now. What can possibly be stopping you?"

The fox opened his mouth, but only a spluttering gasp came out, as if he were being strangled. He tried again, with the same result. *"I . . . I can't . . ."*

Jack didn't reply. He was beginning to feel numb, the

sensation spreading from his core outwards, pushing the heat from him. He wanted to get up and leave Inari in the dust. The fox usually showed up at the most unwanted times, but when he was needed he was so rarely there.

Even as these emotions began to form into a loud rebuke, they withered and died again. Jack was too tired for this, too exhausted by existence. Too much had gone wrong in the last few hours; there was no point adding to the load.

The fox waited a few seconds. Then he wriggled next to Jack, who absently caressed him. *"I'm sorry I can't be of more help. I know it must be difficult at the moment."*

Jack exhaled slowly. "I just don't know what I'm supposed to do. It seems like a huge revelation, but I'm just where I was before. So I can speak any language. Now what? I'm supposed to be leading the Light against the Darkness. How's being multilingual going to help me do that?"

"Far more than you know."

"Can't you give me any more than that?"

Inari turned his triangular head toward him. *"You're on the right track."*

"What, you mean finding the Shards?"

"Not just that. You were on it long before you came across the Apollonians. You're a good person, Jack. Better than me. And that's what will make all the difference in the end."

Night approached slowly, but when it fell, it was particularly clear. A tapestry of stars hailed the gatherers at the pyre. Nothing was said. Jack was glad of that; he wasn't sure he could have handled any kind of elegy or reminiscence. They waited in solemn silence whilst Adâ and Hakim approached, bearing twin alchemical flames between their palms like lotus flowers. They took up positions at opposite ends. Everything was still. Then they lowered the fires onto the fringes of the wood.

To all the lights glimmering in the heavens, they added another, the sparks spiralling into the night. The blazing pyramid, steadily crackling, marked their shadows into the dust. The cloak wore away, and the dim outline of a figure flickered amidst the flames before being obscured.

Jack didn't look at anyone else. His gaze was fixed on the flames until his vision swam with smoke.

As the fire began to quell, the zöpüta dispersed. A little later, the first Apollonians took their respectful leave. Eventually, only Adâ, Hakim, Charles, and Jack remained.

Charles creaked his wheelchair over to him and spoke softly. "I think it's time we gave Adâ some space."

Jack nodded and turned away. Hakim joined them as they made their slow way back towards the shelter, not speaking a word. Jack was glad of the darkness. His eyes had begun to sting, no longer with the heat of the fire.

They hadn't reached the shelter before Lucy became discernible out of the gloom. She was in their path, and it was clear she was there for a purpose. Jack glanced over his shoulder. Adâ was knelt before the embers, her form blurred on the edges by the sinking heat. He didn't want to talk to Lucy right now.

"Jack," she began.

He halted, and the other two continued on their

way. He was left facing the girl with whom he hadn't spoken since his failed attempt just after arriving here. Now didn't seem like the best time.

"Jack, we need to talk . . ."

Jack leaned against the tree and exhaled slowly. They had found a secluded place away from the main shelter, and Lucy had been talking solidly for almost half an hour—it was as if all the time she normally would have spoken to him in the last few weeks came out in one go. She started from the beginning, recounting their arrival at the goblin camp in the Sveta Mountains, meeting Maht and her daughter, their journey to the Cave of Lights, and their capture by the Cult. She had broken down at several points, her eyes shimmering with tears in the distant firelight. And she had finished with a quiet declaration that had left him reeling: she wanted to go home.

"I don't expect you to come with me at all. You're happy here. You've got . . ." She sounded as though she were about to say Ruth but quickly corrected herself. "*People* here who really care about you."

"They care about you just as much as me!"

"Maybe, but still . . . my mum and dad . . . and everyone else . . ."

Jack didn't reply. He couldn't fault Lucy for wanting to go back to her family, not that he knew what that was like.

"And, Jack," she continued, "I don't want to end up like Alex."

The last word was a knife to the stomach, a mingling of pain and guilt. He hadn't *forgotten* about his friend, but with everything else that had gone on, Alex had been pushed to the recesses of his mind. In the chaotic jumble of their time on Nexus, his original reason for being there had momentarily slipped away. Moreover, where was he now? Had he suffered the same fate as all the others who'd been dragged into the void?

"Alex will have got away," Lucy said. "We managed it, so I'm sure he could. He was the one who always looked after *us*, remember?"

"Yeah. Yeah, you're right." He didn't feel as confident as he tried to sound. Like Bál back on Albion, he realized, there was literally no way of knowing what had become of Alex.

"Do you understand now?"

Jack nodded vaguely. He supposed, on reflection, that Lucy's wanting to return to Earth wasn't odd at all. The two of them, after all, had first been pulled into the world of the Apollonians and the Cult by accident. Being taken to Thorin Salr had been for their own safety, not of their own volition. With the Cult gone, it was logical that now was the time she'd choose to go back. From what had become of Bál, of Alex, of Sardâr, he suddenly realized how incredibly fortunate he and Lucy had been to come out with only a few minor injuries. He hadn't even *considered* the possibility of going back to Birchford to take up his old life—but then, Lucy had always had a better time of it than he had. It just seemed shocking that, after so long together, they were going to part ways for an indefinite amount of time.

Lucy didn't seem to know how to proceed. After a moment, she added, very quietly, "Please don't try and stop me."

Jack allowed his eyes to shut; in this darkness, it made little difference either way. "I won't."

Lucy placed her hand on his. "Thank you."

She didn't waste any time about it. They went back to the shelter, where she took Charles aside and explained the situation to him. She said she didn't want to cause a scene, especially considering the cremation, so she would leave overnight and allow others to pass the message around. Vince agreed to take her home.

Before long, she had collected her sparse belongings. As Vince readied one of the dimension ships, the very same turquoise one that had taken them from Earth in the first place, Lucy stowed her sack of clothes in the cargo area.

Jack was the only other one there. "Have you thought how you're going to explain this back home? We must've been gone a good two months now."

"The Apollonians said when we'd left they'd explain to my parents. I guess I'll just have to work with whatever they told them."

When Vince finished the preparations, Lucy turned back to Jack. She was caught between the glow of the fire from the shelter and the whirring lights of the ship's control board. She and Jack stood motionless. Then Lucy ducked into a fleeting hug and retreated to the passenger bench of the ship.

The wings began to vibrate.

Jack's last glimpse was of the grubby, auburn-framed face of his friend, before she was hurtled off in a blaze of lights and darkness.

Chapter XIII
last rites

Hakim had called a private meeting aboard the command deck of *The Golden Turtle*. None of the normal crew members were present, and those who were spoke quietly in a closed circle around the map table: Jack, Dannie, Ruth, Hakim, Adâ, Vince, Gaby, Malik, Charles, and the set of others previously unknown to Jack.

In comparison to the bubbling of the zöpütan dinner, the atmosphere had quelled considerably. It was less than twenty-four hours since the cremation, and everyone was understandably reserved. Hakim and Adâ had come in wearing black. Adâ, he noticed, had also cut her hair: streaming dark locks had been sheared, exposing her frail neck. She looked as if she hadn't slept.

When everyone was assembled, Hakim cleared

his throat, and the mumbling quieted. His voice was cracked but steady. "I'm not going to attempt to elegize Sardâr now. I couldn't do him justice in so few words. Suffice it to say, Adâ and I want to escort his ashes back to Tâbesh. He has no remaining family, but many friends and colleagues are there who will want to honor him. By the laws of our country every citizen, even if they are exiled, has the right to return in death."

There was general nodding around the circle. No one was going to prevent such a reasonable request. Hakim half-turned to Adâ, as if to see if she had anything to add, but she stared absently ahead.

No one said anything for a few moments. The morning sun blazed through the glass dome, catching swirling jets of dust in its beams. No one seemed to want to continue talking.

"I'm presuming, then," Hakim continued, "that the rest of you will remain here until we return?"

"I think so," Charles confirmed, once several people had given their assent. "The zöpüta still have a considerable way to go with their new community, and we can all lend a hand."

Hakim smiled faintly. Jack could tell he was glad that he and Adâ wouldn't be missed too much. "In that case, has anyone got anything more to add?"

Again no one spoke. Jack's heart quickened. He was in a moment of indecision. He knew it was right that the others should know what Sardâr had told him, but this didn't seem like a particularly respectful time. He didn't want to hijack the situation. And yet, they would be angry later if he hadn't told them when they were *all* here . . .

"Well, in that case—"

"I've got something to say." Jack stepped forward slightly. Everyone was now looking at him. He gathered a deep breath, taking in all their waiting expressions, and then took the plunge. "I'm the Übermensch."

He had expected something radical to change. It didn't. Everyone looked at him as if he'd just announced what he'd be having for lunch.

Conscious that he only had a limited time before his credibility completely deserted him, he pressed on. "I can speak all your languages. Literally all of them. Isaac thought that was meant to be a sign, didn't he?"

"Jack," Hakim began, with the tone of one dealing with a delusional child, "as impressive as that is, I'm not sure—"

"No, you don't understand. This is *new.*" He pulled the defunct language ring out of his pocket and held it up to the light. It reminded him of having to stand up and speak in front of a class at school, and the painful memories of that occasion spurred him on. "When I first met you, when this first started, I couldn't speak anything other than English. Now, though, the ring doesn't have any effect."

"He's right." Adâ's voice drew everyone's attention. "He couldn't speak any other languages when we first picked him up."

There was a pause. Jack saw Hakim and Charles exchange skeptical looks. He was losing his audience. Impulsively, he yanked the cord of the Seventh Shard from around his neck and held it at arm's length. "Look, if you don't believe me, watch this. Come on out, Inari."

There was a flash of incandescent light, and a couple of people cried out. It faded, and on the ground beneath the dangling Shard, the double-tailed white fox sat on his hind legs, regarding the room.

"Everyone, this is Inari. Say hello, Inari."

"Hello, everyone," the fox drawled.

Everyone else looked stunned. There was definitely no skepticism now.

"Inari's the one who gave me the Seventh Shard, back on Earth. He's pulled me out of quite a few scrapes so far."

"But," Ruth ventured, "it's a fox . . ."

Inari bristled. *"I'd rather you didn't pander such essentialisms around, my dear. I have two tails, I'm glowing, and I can speak. I am demonstrably not a fox."*

Ruth didn't seem too happy with the rebuke.

"But, more to the point, Jack is the Übermensch, although your terms of reference are hardly fitting. It's more a state of becoming than a state of being."

Dannie seemed to be on a different wavelength. "Does it live *in* the Shard, then?"

"In a manner of speaking. There's no proper mortal equivalent. I suppose I'm tied to the Shard but free to come and go as I please. You'll find that the other Shards are similarly inhabited, although because of some special conditions you won't find any of their denizens as vocal as I. And, madam, I'd also rather you addressed me directly, rather than through Jack. Really, you lot call yourselves civilized."

Jack thought it was time to intervene. "Okay, Inari, that's enough."

The fox did its equivalent of rolling its eyes, and a moment later it had vanished.

There was a stunned silence.

"Sardâr worked it out originally," Jack said, wanting to acknowledge the real source. "He said he'd had his suspicions for a while, but . . ."

"So if he's the Übermensch," Dannie began slowly, "then that's good, isn't it?"

"Very much so," Hakim replied weakly. "All we need to do is find the remaining Shards, and . . ." He let the remainder of his sentence hang.

Jack continued. "Well, I was thinking about that. We're fairly sure there's a Shard in this world, aren't we? And now that the Cult's gone, it's not going to be at all as risky to find it. There aren't any people besides us: the worst we'll come across are a few wild animals. I could take a dimension ship with a few others and bring it back here, whilst Hakim and Adâ are away. Then we can sort out what to do about the others after that."

He hoped he sounded sincere. Of course, he *was* planning to go and get the Shard, but Lucy's departure had given him a jolting reminder of the real reason he'd become involved with the Apollonians in the first place: to find Alex. And if Alex had been on Nexus, there was a good chance he would have ended up somewhere on this planet—if he'd managed to get out at all.

"That seems reasonable." Charles nodded along with several others. "We haven't thought about the implications of the Cult being gone yet, but it would seem that the pursuit of the Shard will now be considerably easier.

Who would you take with you? If it's to be one of our ordinary dimension ships, then it can't be a big group."

Jack looked around the assembled faces. He knew who he wanted but was tentative about announcing it to the group. He was saved the embarrassment when Ruth stepped forward.

"I'm in."

"Me too," Dannie added, rolling the Third Shard between finger and thumb. "Sounds like you could use someone with another one of these. Mine's got a shiny animal as well, then?"

"Three's fine," Jack said quickly. He didn't want the entire group volunteering, or it would turn into something like a school trip.

Preparations didn't take long. Their trio was allocated one of the other dimension ships: very like the one Lucy had been taken home in but violet instead of turquoise. Their belongings and some provisions were loaded in the cargo section beneath, including an egg from *The Golden Turtle* for contact purposes.

As they were stocking up the ship, Adâ approached. Jack panicked slightly: he had avoided speaking to her since Sardâr's death, not knowing how to possibly begin consoling her.

However, she didn't seem to expect him to say anything. She was holding an object that he initially took to be a slab of stone, but he realized it was the Cultist mirror they'd taken from Thorin Salr. The surface was now dulled completely. It had lost its obsidian quality and now seemed as if it could have slid out of any cliff face.

280

She pressed it into the crook of one of his arms. "It might come in useful."

He scrabbled for something to say. "I know you'll make sure he's sent off properly." The words sounded painfully blasé.

Adâ didn't seem to mind. Instead, she pulled him into a brief hug. "Look after yourselves. He cared about you."

The zöpüta brought gifts for them as well. Along with drying foods, they had been experimenting with art. They presented Jack, Ruth, and Dannie wallet-sized woven sculptures in the likeness of lion heads. Jack clipped his onto the thread around his neck to hang with the Seventh Shard, whilst Ruth planted hers in her hair. Dannie, after a failed attempt to eat hers, sheepishly deposited it in one of the pouches on her belt.

They were ready within half an hour. Ruth was in the pilot's position, adjusting controls, whilst Dannie looked on with interest. The remaining Apollonians had collected by the side of the ship, along with an assortment of zöpüta.

Charles wheeled over, and Jack crouched on the edge of the ship to hear him speak. "I know this should be straightforward, but don't get complacent. We've survived the wreckage of Nexus, so others may have too."

Jack nodded and was about to stand.

Charles halted him, speaking more discreetly. "And watch out for that fox."

"Inari's always been—"

"I know you trust him," Charles pressed on, "and perhaps with good reason. But I'm sure you remember as well as I do what Isaac's last letter said about a white fox."

"Okay, we're ready," Ruth called.

Jack backed away and strapped himself in with the odd jellied belts as Charles cleared the vicinity. The vibrations from below and the suddenly blurring air around them told him that the wings had begun to beat. He saw that Dannie hadn't bothered to put hers on. "Trust me," he told her. "Use that. You didn't see what happened to Vince . . ."

The two passengers had just begun to wave as Ruth slammed her palm down on the control panel. The ship lurched forwards, and they caught a last glimpse of waving figures, the shelters, and the metallic sheen of *The Golden Turtle* before they were hurtling across the savannah under the beating sun.

Chapter XIV
chthonia

The first hints of spring brushed the orchard. The bare-branched trees, marked against the pale morning sky like candelabras, glimmered with their first few leaves. The air was cold, colder than in Nduino, though certainly nowhere near that of the Sveta Mountains. A few birds called out—not condors or vultures or any recognizable equivalent, but normal, British birds.

They were on top of Sirona Beacon. Metal railings, screened off by flapping canvas, had been erected all around the hilltop, blocking the view beyond. The gondola-style dimension ship was tilted slightly, having hewn a line in the ground upon landing. It had come to rest next to a large circle of earth that looked as if it had been newly turned or something had been buried beneath.

Vince stood aboard, Lucy on the grass. It was, she remembered, almost exactly the same place on the hill she had been held captive by the Cult that night when everything had changed.

Her appearance was incongruous at best. *The Golden Turtle*'s stock of clothing had been diminished significantly by the refugees, so the options hadn't been good. What she had come out with was hardly adequate: a dragon-woven dressing gown that trailed at her feet, pantaloons which swelled her upper thighs to the size of watermelons, a ruffled silk shirt, and a hat that may once have been fashionable but, inexplicably, had a stuffed koala-type creature attached to its brim. On top of that, she was trying to balance a bundle of furs that had come from the goblin camp, making her look like she'd grown a gigantic beard. She hadn't even begun to think how she was going to explain this.

"So this is it?" Vince said. He seemed intent on containing his laughter.

"I guess so." Lucy's reply was muffled by the furs. Now here, she was unsure of what to say. Being escorted home on a flying gondola after a trip around the universe didn't exactly have a precedent.

"Take care of yourself. And take this." He tossed her something.

She caught it, dropping several furs in the process. Turning it over, she saw that it was one of the clasped eggs from *The Golden Turtle*.

"This thing can't change clothes, can it?"

Vince finally broke into chuckles. "Unfortunately not. Keep it, just in case."

She paused, then nodded and tucked it into one of the dressing gown pockets.

Vince smiled and climbed down into the control position of the ship. He adjusted a few controls, and it flashed into life. "Good luck!"

The paneled wings of the ship began to judder and became blurred, lifting it into the air. The last sight she saw was Vince turning a dial, and then with an echoing sonic boom, the entire structure vanished into thin air.

She waited for a moment. Everything was still. Then she dropped the furs and began to strip off layers. The pantaloons had to go, and the hat, and the ridiculous high-topped boots she'd forced her legs into. Her bare feet sunk into the dewy grass. It was cold, but it was necessary. She still knew very little about what her parents had been told about her absence, so she had to be prepared for any reaction they might have to her walking semiclothed through the front door as if nothing had happened.

She had turned down Vince's offer to come and explain things. Before her disappearance, her dad would probably have called the police if she had come home with a boy. Combine that with her lengthy absence, and he might have had a seizure. There was also the matter of Vince himself. He was several years older and, to put it lightly, not the kind of person her parents would be happy with her being around. It had taken her a long time to convince them that Jack, living in a state-funded orphanage, wasn't a waste of taxpayer's money. Amongst the Apollonians Vince was a freedom fighter, but she knew her family would immediately caricature him as a rowdy, drug-addicted benefit scrounger.

She paused, wondering whether she'd forgotten anything. She felt the egg in her pocket and pulled it out. The burnished metal caught the light, reflecting a distorted version of her face. She considered it, then let it drop onto the pile of disused clothes on the grass.

Wrapping the dressing gown closer to her, she began trudging down the hill.

Alex returned to consciousness. The ground beneath him was wet. His body ached all over, and he was sure he was bleeding from somewhere: he still wore his tunic, but it was in tatters and heavy with brine. Mustering his energy, he cracked open his eyelids and pulled himself to his feet.

He seemed to be on a beach. Behind him, some kind of immense lake or ocean opened out—entirely silent, save for the lapping against his heels. In front, a gorge of pitiless ashen rock led uphill. The sky was like nothing he'd ever seen. It was splintered between light and darkness: behind him, white fog; in front, a bank of obsidian brewing on the horizon.

He was not alone. A tall, grey figure stood a few feet before him, facing away.

"Where are we?" Alex spluttered, his lungs ejecting a layer of sour water.

"At the end of the universe. Chthonia, where the Light meets the Darkness."

Alex tried to remember. He had seen the indigo light from his room and done as he was instructed. He had concentrated, and Darkness had bloomed before him, a portal into nothingness. He had stepped inside and felt himself slip away in black smoke. He had hurtled through oblivion, his individuality almost consumed, and lost consciousness. The last thing he could remember was a grey presence speeding alongside, carrying him away from some cataclysm behind.

"You're not the Emperor, are you?"

The grey figure turned. "No. The Emperor was a tool: a mortal vessel, consumed by fanaticism. He is gone, along with Nexus and the Cult of Dionysus."

"So what *are* you?" Alex demanded. Despite his mental and physical exhaustion, he could feel the rage rising up again. He could feel the power he had become so used to surging through him, alighting on every particle of blood in his veins. He was a conduit—something had ripped open inside him, and unfettered energy swooped out. He could feel more than see now. His outstretched arms shook with the force of obsidian fire blasting outwards. He had been imprisoned for months by the grey *thing*, but no more. *No more.*

The grey figure remained motionless, the flames brushing him ineffectually. His expression was unreadable, but those golden orbs burnt through the inferno, brighter and more terrible than the rolling flames.

Alex's rage subsided, and the energy ebbed. He was gasping heavily, beads of burning sweat seeping from his scalp.

The figure appraised him with those twin jewels, set in a statue of wilting rock. "I am not the one you should be venting your anger at. It was your so-called friends who left you for dead. They came to Nexus the night it was destroyed. They liberated others—humans, elves, even the natives—but not you."

"Liar," Alex shouted, flecks of spittle wetting the pebbles. "They weren't there. They'd never leave me."

For the first time, the figure smirked. "Perhaps you value them too highly."

And with a deadening thud, the object dropped to the ground before Alex. He felt the heat drain from him entirely. There was no mistaking the object before him: a dull metal egg held in curved clasps, taken from the heart of *The Golden Turtle.* So the Apollonians *had* been to Nexus and had not come to find him. There was no question as to whether they'd known he was there. They'd all seen him vanishing into the Darkness with Icarus.

He dropped to his knees, his eyes searing with tears. The void that had opened within him sparked once more: rage, not at this grey figure or his predicament, but at his friends' betrayal. He had stayed strong, he had stayed loyal, and it had all been for nothing.

He screwed up his eyes and roared into the silent day-night, feeling the flames burst anew around him. He was an anti-sun, Dark energy shooting outwards in convulsions of anger and hatred.

When the flames finally quelled, his chest was heaving again. He opened his eyes. The rocks and cliffs were scorched black, indigo embers kindling in the cracks. The grey figure was gone, leaving the ashen path curling upwards before him.

And, though he could not see it, his eyes were no longer emerald green but bright, burning gold.

MEDALLION
P R E S S

Be in the know on the latest Medallion Press news
by becoming a Medallion Press Insider!

<u>As an Insider you'll receive:</u>
· Our FREE expanded monthly newsletter, giving you more insight
into Medallion Press
· Advanced press releases and breaking news
· Greater access to all your favorite Medallion authors

Joining is easy. Just visit our website at
<u>www.medallionmediagroup.com</u> and click on
Super Cool E-blast next to the social media buttons.

MEDALLION
P R E S S

Want to know what's going on with your favorite author or
what new releases are coming from Medallion Press?

Now you can receive breaking news, updates, and more from
Medallion Press straight to your cell phone, e-mail, instant messenger,
or Facebook!

Sign up now at www.twitter.com/MedallionPress to stay on top
of all the happenings in and around Medallion Press.

For more information
about other great titles from
Medallion Press, visit

medallionmediagroup.com